By Aaron Marc Stein

THE GARBAGE COLLECTOR

AARON MARC STEIN

PUBLISHED FOR THE CRIME CLUB BY
DOUBLEDAY & COMPANY, INC.
GARDEN CITY, NEW YORK
1984

All of the characters in this book
are fictitious, and any resemblance
to actual persons, living or dead,
is purely coincidental.

Library of Congress Cataloging in Publication Data
Stein, Aaron Marc, 1906–
The garbage collector.
I. Title.
PS3537.T3184G3   1984   813'.52   84-6044
ISBN 0-385-19484-6

For the learned Doctors Alicia Butcher Ehrhardt and Bill Ehrhardt in gratitude for the assistance they gave the author in the taming of his word processor

THE GARBAGE
COLLECTOR

CHAPTER 1

It was beautiful. The view I had from my terrace could almost make me forget that it was the land of cheese and chocolate, of clockwork and cash, and see it as a place of romance and brave deeds, of Wilhelm Tell and the Prisoner of Chillon.

When the sun was on the lake, it was pretty. There was the background of mountains with their high-held peaks brushed white by the lustrous clouds, there were the sailboats with striped sails.

When the great storms struck it, however, it was magnificent. I would watch the clouds mass at the mountaintops. Rolling like tumbleweed down the slopes, they would fatten as they came. In moments it would be a world transformed, a world that retreated behind wind-whipped curtains of rain while it changed its face to a menacing scowl. Thunder and wind howl obliterated all lesser sound, and great whips of lightning lashed the lake. It was at such times that a man's romantic fancies ran riot.

Such fancies were also nourished by my dwelling place. I had this lakeside flat which I rented furnished among those in a great stone building designed to withstand a siege and which had done no less on several occasions in medieval times. It had been the granary in which the Dukes of Savoy had stored their grain against the years of famine, when they could unload it on the starving masses at the sort of prices that had brought on the French Revolution.

The building had been gutted and its interior had been modernized, but its marble bathtubs, its ultramodern kitchens, and its electrical wiring had taken nothing away from its impregnability. Just across the road rose the battlemented walls of the old bastard's castle. In that setting it was easy to imagine that my generously haunched and paunched neighbors were not Geneva financiers fresh from a killing on the Bourse, but Crusaders newly returned from looting Byzantium, and that the cars parked outside were not the Jaguar and the Mercedes, the BMW and the Rolls that they appeared to be, but fully caparisoned steeds of war eager to enter the jousting lists. I had never taken my Porsche anywhere where she was more taken for granted. Here Baby was just another among her peers. You cannot expect me to say among her betters. Of those she has none.

These mountain storms are likely to blow themselves out as quickly as they build themselves up. Tonight's storm, however, came up about a half hour before sunset and it was full dark before it had spent itself. It was only after the rain had stopped and the fall had been reduced to nothing more than the dripping from the eaves that I could begin to recognize how deeply it was night. The last rumble of thunder had faded; the last lightning flash had flickered out.

There was nothing but silence and black night. Across the lake was the taunt of lights shining in Switzerland. On my side, in France, we had no light at all. Their storm had knocked out our power lines. I groped my way to a closet where I remembered seeing a flashlight. Armed with that, I went on a hunt for candles.

My thoughtful landlord had left me two minute candle stubs to light me through such emergencies. That they had been fancy candles molded to elaborate shapes now distorted by deluges of drippings was only too characteristic of the man whose kitchen could boast a duck press but no coffeepot of any description. There was nothing for it but a quick run to the next village for a supply of candles. That much I had learned about my village at first sight. Eight kilometers from the Swiss border and fifteen from Geneva, it was nothing more than a dormitory town for the haunched and paunched of that city. There were no stores. For even the simplest emergency shopping it was the seven kilometers out to the little market in the neighboring hamlet.

Armed with the flashlight, I headed down to the Porsche. She was parked about fifty yards down the road—everything nearer had been preempted by my neighbors. Her parking place was at the corner of the castle wall, alongside which a path cut away to skirt it. This was narrow, nowhere wide enough to take a car, just a footpath that gave access to a shortcut out to the main road. Like the roads in the town it was surfaced with gravel; the main road had a hard surface. As I crossed the mouth of the footpath, I heard the voice and the accompanying sounds. The voice was a muffled growl but not difficult to understand. It said: "Merde." Anyone could have inferred "merde" from its tone.

That made it easy. The accompanying sounds were a bump followed by a shuffling scrape of gravel. Somebody was in the footpath doing a poor job of feeling his way. Brimming over with sympathy and fellow feeling, I turned the beam of my flashlight into the alley. I was without curiosity. This would be another victim of an inconsiderate or impractical landlord. He was caught in the blackout without a candle and a little help was indicated. No ex–Boy Scout could do less.

Immediately, however, I did develop some curiosity, but it was not to be satisfied that night. As soon as I'd swung the beam toward the footpath, the shots came. The first two were near-misses, which came in rapid fire. The third zeroed in on the target. I was now as much without light as anyone, and quite as much in the mood for growling "Merde."

I would like to have done several things about it, but none of them were wise. So I slid behind Baby's wheel and asked her to give me everything she had, and we got ourselves away from there. I was trying to recall who it had been back in the days of my innocence who had told me that Boy

Scout training would be a good preparation for life. There was a guy who should have been put wise to a few things.

As I drove, I worked at cooling myself down. I was telling myself it could have been worse. I had come out of the encounter unnicked, and Baby had also survived without a scratch. There was, of course, one ruined flashlight, but it would not be difficult to replace. All my instincts, however, told me not to replace it. Surely it was exactly what my landlord needed, a flashlight more decorative than useful, to go with the candle stubs. I drove the seven kilometers and bought the candles. By that time it seemed to me that I owed myself a reward for my self-restraint and sober good sense. I went on another eight kilometers to a café where over a cognac I could swap tales of the night's storm damage and swap shots in the dark at the significance of the shots in the dark.

It was the consensus that I had offered my unwelcome assistance to a burglar.

On this side of the border they were the Swiss villains; across the line they would have been the French malefactors. The little stone houses in my lakeside village had been restored, furnished, modernized, and equipped most expensively. Their owners occupied them only on weekends and over holidays, and burglars hit them regularly on dark midweek nights. They had been hitting them with even greater regularity ever since the price of silver had been zooming upward. It was the accepted my-thology that my locality was far more lavishly fur-nished with burglars than any other neighborhood. They were all the bastard descendants of the old dukes.

I had hardly started down the road back to the lake when the power returned and I was able to park Baby without running her afoul of the shat-tered glass from the flashlight. There was a good light fixed to the castle wall at the mouth of the footpath. I kicked the broken glass to one side, clearing it off the road. Then I spotted the empty shell cases. I picked them up. There were just the three of them. The guy carried heavy artillery. The fire I had been under had not come from any toy.

I explored the full length of the path and saw nobody. It seemed as though everyone had surren-dered to the blackout and gone to bed early. It seemed a good idea.

I went upstairs to the flat and turned in. I fully expected that the morning would bring its full quota of tales of the overnight depredations of the marauding Swiss. This would be coming from the local woman who kept the flat clean and filled the freezer with the meals she cooked for me to warm for myself. Nothing could happen between the lake and the Swiss border without my Mme Douvaine hearing of it. She was a specialist on illegitimacy and infidelity, but minor irregularities were not permitted to go unremarked either.

That morning the irregularity seemed to be most

minor, even though she was prone to give it high marks in the scandal department. The garbage man had not been around to do his semi-weekly pickup. The trash stood untouched on the doorsteps. It was beginning to stink. The public health was in peril. The taxpayers were being cheated. The pigs were being deprived. The flies and the rats were beginning to congregate. Honest men could count on nothing anymore.

I was taking my breakfast out on the terrace. It was an established part of my daily routine. Every morning I had guests come to share my breakfast croissant: every morning a duck and drake would bring their troop of small *farceurs* to breakfast with me. Then a little later, when I would be lighting up with my second cup of coffee, there would be the second sitting—or perhaps more properly, the second floating. It would be a pair of swans, stately and aloof, with their brood of cygnets. They adhered strictly to schedule, except that this one morning in both cases they came, they looked, and they beat a hasty retreat. This was mystifying behavior. I could only think that some particularly horrid and terrifying predator had invaded the territory and was down there fattening on my largesse.

I went to the rail and looked over. There was something down there, but it was not a predator and it threatened nothing. It was certainly well beyond having any interest in croissants. When my cleaning woman joined me at the terrace rail, however, it appeared to have on her the same effect it had on the ducks and the swans. She recoiled from it and she trembled. She had rituals unknown to the water birds and she had resort to them. She crossed herself. She mumbled a rapid succession of Hail Marys. She asked the garbage man's forgiveness. Even from up on the terrace the identification was unmistakable: it was the garbage collector and he was dead.

"Drowned in the storm," I said, but I wasn't believing a word of it.

The man had been a boatman who'd spent his life on the water. He was like the lake perch or the waterfowl—the lake was his element. This had been a man who would have been more at peril on the little-traveled roads of the village than he ever could have been on the water. There had been times when I would be out on my terrace with a drink during the lingering twilights of the long summer evenings. At those moments I had seen the garbage collector go about his job, moving with the most surefooted ease between the boat landings and the deck of his garbage scow. It was not possible that he could have slipped and fallen into the water; but even then it would have been even less possible for him to have been unable to keep himself afloat in even the wildest of Alpine tempests.

I left the cleaning woman to her panicky devotions and ran downstairs for a closer look at the body. On the way I noticed that the garbage had been set out at all the apartment doors and hadn't been touched. I could guess that disaster had over-taken the collector in the midst of his pickup. His regular route took him along the lakefront from west to east. I looked over at the house next door. It was obvious that the storm had not interfered with his making his regular rounds. He had done his pickup there; all their garbage bags had been re-moved.

Down at the edge of the boat landing I could learn nothing. Looking down into the water, I could see that the man was dead, gone beyond any hope of reviving. I had seen that much, however, from the terrace. If on the landing there had been any clue to how he had come there, the sluicing rain of the big storm had washed it all away.

There was nothing for it but to call the police. But since one of the amenities furnished to me by my most peculiar landlord was a lock on the tele-phone, I had to go to the village post office to make my call.

One of the prerogatives that went with the post-master's job was listening in on all telephone con-versations. Any such sophisticated device as a tele-phone tap would have been an extravagantly wasteful gadget. One needed only to ask the post-master.

He found my talk with the police most unsatis-factory. It raised too many questions and provided too few answers. This would be a most absurd crime. If there was ever a man who had no ene-mies, it was the garbage collector. He was without money and without possessions. He only barely owned the pants he stood up in, and even those were a pair he had scavenged out of the garbage. There was his garbage scow, of course, but what manner of pirate would pass up all the beautiful sailboats the rich raced on the lake to snatch the garbage scow? It wasn't sensible. So what could be left to move a man to murder? Jealousy? How could a man who smelled so bad be a threat to the virtue of any man's wife or daughter? It was impossible.

The police were less difficult to convince. They may not have believed murder, but they were not disposed to doubt sudden death. I returned to the boat landing to wait for them.

On the way back, I noticed another oddity. The guy in the house next door—the last house along the lakefront to have had a garbage pickup—owned the kind of cabin cruiser used by heads of state. The evening before the storm it had been tethered securely to his boat landing, sitting in the water precisely as it did on weekdays. Now it was secured in the same way but you would hardly know it was the same boat. It had taken a battering. Its paintwork was scraped and soiled. Never before had it shown so much as the slightest scratch.

Far greater damage might have been expected in a storm of such violence? No. It had been far too well-tethered and far too thoroughly protected, hung as it was with collision mats. The sides of the landing had been similarly festooned, and all of this protective padding was still there, undisturbed. The storm hadn't battered the boat against the dock. Someone had had it out during the storm and had been joyriding in it.

I strolled out to the dock and called out a greeting. There was no answer. The house appeared to be securely buttoned up. With all the blinds drawn, the windows were blank. Everything seemed to be in its normal midweek condition. It would be this way until early Friday, when the servants came to open up the house and take the deliveries from the Geneva gourmet shops. Friday afternoon it would come to life with tea and drinks on the boat dock. The host would lead his guests in a bout of the merry sport of windsurfing, in which the victory seemed to go to the player who could make the quickest and splashiest landing on his fat ass; any success at remaining upright appeared to be against the rules.

I jumped to the deck of the cruiser. Its rain-soaked planks were steaming in the sun, but one area of deck, sheltered under a canopy, had never been touched by the rain. It had been touched by blood instead.

The spoor was easily followed. It was a clear trail that led into the cabin. Taking great care not to step in it, I followed where it led. Inside, the cabin was in a moderate state of disorder. A couple of blood-smeared bath towels had been dropped to the floor, and a pair of cinnamon-colored slacks of unbelievable dimensions lay there with them. The slacks were also bloodied, as was a butter-yellow silk shirt. Had this fattest of fat men been to a pig sticking? I went back to the landing and, while waiting for the police, I thought.

The garbage pickups had come this far and then stopped. But a house that has been locked up and unoccupied for several days generates no garbage. Nevertheless, I distinctly remembered having seen sacks on the boat landing the previous afternoon before the storm. They had been lined up and waiting for collection just as they might have been on a Sunday evening. Now that I was thinking about it, it had been curiously early.

Ordinarily on a Sunday night it would have waited until much later, until after the host had taken off with the last of his guests and the servants had finished cleaning the place and securing it until the invasion that would come with the next weekend. I hadn't thought of any of that at the time, but then again how much thought is a man likely to give to garbage?

The village was too small to rate even one police officer. My friend the postmaster was its sole representative of officialdom. The nearest gendarmerie was in that larger town fifteen kilometers away, out on the highway. Considering the distance and a force that couldn't have been heavily manned, the response to my call was quick and impressive. Crime had invaded the peaceful enclave that belonged to the rich and the privileged. It was not to be countenanced. The honor of Socialist France hung on it.

I met the gendarmes and guided them down to the boat landing to the place where the body floated. After taking the necessary photographs, they fished it out of the water. It presented that all too usual picture: the back of the head had that mushily misshapen look heads take on when they have been sufficiently battered with the proverbial blunt instrument. The cold water of the lake had pretty well stopped the bleeding, but it was obvious that the loss of blood had been considerable, quite enough to account for the trail of it that led into the boat cabin and for the staining of the shirt, slacks, and towels.

CHAPTER 2

"What do you know about this unfortunate affair, M. Erridge?"

"No more than I can see."

"But you were crying murder before we had him out of the water, and it could be seen."

"I had watched the man work. He was a good man around boats and he was a strong swimmer. Such men do not have accidents."

"It was a heavy storm last night."

"Heavy enough to mess up the cabin cruiser next door."

They looked at the cruiser. They expressed dismay and disapproval. A boat so beautiful ought to be better cared for. This was not a boat to be neglected.

"It never has been, before this," I said.

"Why do you speak of it, M. Erridge?"

"The man was on it before he was dumped in the water."

"You saw him? You witnessed it?"

"There was nothing to see last night but rain and lightning. It was impossible. But you can see for yourselves—on the boat."

They went aboard and explored. I had expected gratitude, but I should have known better. After all, they hadn't asked me to do their work for them.

"What do you know about this affair, M. Erridge?"

"What I can see," I said, and then immediately I thought better of it. "No," I said, "there's a little more than that."

"Ah. That's better. You must tell us everything."

"It isn't much, except that yesterday under cover of the storm something was going on around here. I haven't a clue to what it was except that I do know it was something violent."

"And how can you know that, M. Erridge?"

"I was shot at," I said. "Where I come from that is not considered friendly."

"So? And what have you done to make yourself such an enemy? Why should there be someone here who would want to kill you? We don't have killings here. This is not Chicago. . . . What do you know about Henri-Edouard de Montbard?"

"Who's he?"

"You are telling us that you don't know him?"

"Never heard of him."

"You make yourself at home on his boat."

"He the tub who owns this tub? I see him from my terrace. He's too fat, too rich, and too loud-mouthed. Anything else you want to know?"

"Yes, M. Erridge. Why are you here? What are you doing in this village?"

"I prefer not to live in Switzerland. I've never before known the French to be inhospitable."

"Henri-Edouard de Montbard has a wife."

"On the weekends I see many women here."

"Mathilde de Montbard is very beautiful. She has many lovers, but he consoles himself well."

"Bully for him."

"You're living alone?"

"It is convenient."

"In what way convenient?"

"For being close to Switzerland."

"And when ladies come to visit."

"I suppose so; but it's wasted on a man who's taken the vow of chastity."

The gendarmes paid me the compliment of taking that with a large dose of incredulity. But even though I was prepared to take into consideration the fact that they were French, I found it difficult to understand why they should be so much more interested in my sex life than they were in the gunfire I had drawn the previous evening.

The body was removed and I shook loose from the fuzz to hit the road to Geneva and keep my business engagements. To my astonishment the news of the murder of the garbage collector had come there before me. They were talking of nothing else in the banks and in the counting houses. It was the consensus that de Montbard and murder had long been running a collision course. It had been a question only of how long it was to be before it would have come.

"The bastard collected enemies the way a mongrel dog collects fleas. He went through life leaving in his wake a trail of ruined men."

He had robbed and he had cheated. He had fattened on the misfortunes of other men. He had come by his rapacity through inheritance; it had been imprinted on his genes. His father before him had gone into World War II a wealthy man and emerged from it obscenely richer. Never had there been a disaster anywhere that had not somehow put another fortune in de Montbard Sr.'s pocket. Wartime France, wartime Germany, Austria, Czechoslovakia, Poland—wherever there was a loss, it had become in some mysterious way a de Montbard profit.

At war's end de Montbard *père* had stood trial for collaboration, and that had been a narrow squeak— but only insofar as the old man had escaped lynching by almost no margin at all. It had been impossible to prove anything.

"Okay, but what then could the son want with a garbage collector?"

"The police will be looking for the murdered man's wife or daughter. This has always been de Montbard's method. He ruins the husband and adds the wife to his harem. It's been a standard joke in the Geneva clubs that an ugly wife is a man's best defense against him."

"But how could any woman go for the slob?"

"If, say, it's the price of keeping her husband alive . . . or, failing that, it's luxury, security, furs, and diamonds. It beats begging any day."

It was over lunch in one of those Geneva clubs that the talk changed. None of the easy answers was working anymore. The garbage scow had been found around mid-morning. It had been sighted adrift on the lake and had been picked up. On it had been found the great, gross carcass of Henri-Edouard de Montbard. He had taken one revolver slug in the belly, one in the head, and one in the heart.

Someone was performing in triplets. I could expect that the gendarmes would now be less bored with my story of how the flashlight had been shot out of my hand.

It was late afternoon before I'd finished my business and taken the road back across the border to return home. By that time police activity had moved away from the house next door. The cabin cruiser was no longer at its mooring. I could guess that the gendarmes had taken it in for the full laboratory workup. In any event, they couldn't have left it to disfigure our neighborhood. We were far too elegant and luxurious for that.

Inside the fastnesses of my onetime granary the garbage bags had been picked up from outside my apartment door. Apparently some emergency collection had been arranged, and it wasn't a moment too soon. The hallways of the building were beginning to be noticeably malodorous.

My apartment door was hanging slightly ajar. There was something very wrong about that. Mme Douvaine was most particular about keeping it locked. She considered herself to be the guardian of my landlord's store of treasures and she was stern

in her disapproval of what she took to be my care-
less disregard of adequate security. The door was
not equipped with a snap lock. You needed a key to
lock or unlock it. The key was large and heavy, and
keeping it always ready was a nuisance. It was the
sort of sharp-cornered object that is designed to
chew holes in the pockets of a man's pants and the
thing was so ridiculously heavy that it carried the
threat of hauling my pants down around my an-
kles.

I never bothered to keep the door locked when I
was at home and I was always going out and leaving the door unlocked. Mme Douvaine was aware
of this. She let me know as much by locking it and
making it necessary for me to fetch her to open it
up for me. Each time, I was lectured on the need
for security and on my obligation to see to the safe-
guarding of my landlord's property. She would
paint me chilling pictures of her fears of the morning when she would come in to do up the flat and
find me in bed with my throat cut from ear to ear.
Of course we were in France and she conceded that
there was no crime in France, but I was not to
forget that just to the south of us lay Chamonix and
the Mont Blanc tunnel. The other side of the tunnel was Italy, and we all knew what those Italians
were.

Standing back, out of range, I kicked the door
open. I was greeted with total silence.

I could see only dimly since all the blinds were
tightly drawn, but there was nothing unusual

about that. It was the way Madame always left the place: we couldn't permit the sun to shine in—it might fade my landlord's upholstery and rug. I waited a moment to allow my eyes to adjust to the dimness. All over the room things seemed to be where they shouldn't have been. I reached for the wall switch and turned on the lights. The lighting, like almost everything else in the place, was more decorative than useful, but there was just enough reflected glow to show me that I'd had a visitor. I could see well enough to pick my way among the obstacles to reach the window and let the sun in on the chaos. The room had been ransacked, and everything lay in heaps over the floor. Quickly I explored the rest of the place. It was the same everywhere.

Suddenly, it appeared that I was in the midst of a crime wave. I shut the door on it.

On my way down the stairs, as I headed for the telephone, I noticed something I had been overlooking. It was most peculiar. It had to be significant, although I couldn't imagine how. There had been no emergency garbage collection. The bags were still outside all the other doors. Only mine had been removed. It seemed too insane.

I told myself that Mme Douvaine had done the pickup herself. It seemed the most rational answer, but it immediately raised unanswerable questions. Where would she have taken it? How could she have disposed of it? Also, why would she have undertaken it? With the bags still outside all the other

doors and the reek becoming increasingly noticeable, the removal contributed very little toward
sanitation.

As I went rattling down the stairs, Georges
Bardelot, the neighbor who lived in the apartment
below me, opened his door.

"You worked hard this afternoon," he said.

It was the politely veiled approach to asking
about all the noise that had been going on above his
head.

"I have been in Geneva all afternoon," I said. "I
only just got home."

"Then it must have been Mme Douvaine. She
sounded like a wrecking crew."

"It was a wrecking crew. Burglars. I am going
out to phone the police."

"The post office? Use my telephone."

"You are very kind. I suppose you saw no one."

He smiled ruefully. "I'm afraid I made it a point
not to see anyone," he said. "It would have been
impolite."

"It's just as well. The man's dangerous."

"According to the gendarmes, robbers may be
dangerous. Burglars, as a rule, are not."

"Murderers pretty much always are," I said.

"The garbage collector?"

"You haven't heard about the man next door?"

"The mountain of lard? What about him?"

"He was also killed last night. His body was
found adrift on the lake in the garbage scow."

"A murderer with a sense of the appropriate."

I got through to the police and they said they would be right over. They sounded as if they were glad to hear from me. I was wondering whether they could be beginning to look on me as an old friend.

"The gendarmes are on their way. I'd better be back upstairs waiting for them."

"I'll go with you," my neighbor said. "Just give me a moment."

M. Bardelot popped into the bedroom. He was away only the promised moment, and he came back with a gun.

"You won't need that," I said.

"He might still be up there. Can you be sure he isn't?"

"I've been all through the place. He isn't."

"Under the beds? Into the closets?"

"I wasn't that thorough," I admitted.

My neighbor disapproved of me. "You can't be too careful." Outside the door to the flat he stopped. "Your garbage?" he asked. "Has it been picked up or didn't you put any out last night?"

"I put some out."

"And it's been stolen. This is no murderer. This is a lunatic." Inside the flat he surveyed the disorder and whistled.

"You shouldn't be surprised," I said. "You heard him shoving all this stuff around."

"Did he take much?"

"I have no way of knowing. I had nothing much to take, only some clothing and a few books. There

was no money around—that I had on me. As far as
the things that came with the apartment, I really
don't know. Maybe he ended up taking nothing but
the garbage."

It was pretty much the same routine all over
again with the gendarmes. There were the obvious
things—a typewriter, some expensive luggage, the
color TV, an elaborate stereo setup with a most
exquisite discrimination—and an instant check
showed that none of those was missing. In the same
way, although the kitchen drawers and cabinet had
been turned out and their contents strewn around
the kitchen, everything seemed to be there. The
one item of obvious value, the silver, was intact.

"You'll think I'm crazy," I said. "And why not?
I'm thinking so myself. But the only thing I can see
is gone is the garbage."

The gendarmes ignored that. They had something else on their minds.

"You have a gun, M. Erridge."

It wasn't remarkable that they should know,
only that they should have been checking up on
me. In these days of terrorism you can't board a
plane with a gun on you. I had therefore declared
mine, signed all the necessary papers, and surren-
dered it for the duration of the flight. I also had
gone through all the formalities of seeing it
through customs. It was a matter of record.

"Yes," I said. "Properly registered."

"Do you still have it?"

"I don't know. I'll see."

I went into the bedroom to look for it in the drawer of the bedside table, and one of the gendarmes came with me. He was right on top of me all the way. They were taking no chances on my arming myself and going berserk. They were making no secret of it: I was suspect.

I opened the drawer. The gun wasn't there.

"What is their interest in you, M. Erridge?" they asked, on our return.

"I was hoping *you* might tell me that."

"What did you have to do with de Montbard?"

"He was the fat man in the house next door. A couple of times when I would happen to see him out on his boat dock on a weekend morning, I would say 'Good morning' and he would say 'Bonjour.' It's a mistake I make. I talk to everybody."

"This is not the time for the jokes, M. Erridge."

"I am taking it seriously. When I call the police, I'm not joking."

"Your situation is dangerous. Two men have lost their lives."

"And I've lost nothing but my garbage. That is a loss you cannot expect me to take too seriously."

"Your pistol, M. Erridge."

"I must regret that. It means that I will need to depend on you to protect me."

"What is your business in Geneva?"

"I am an engineer. There is to be a dam, and the financing will be Swiss."

"Out of a secret account?"

"It is nowhere in my contract that I must know where the money comes from."

"Swiss financing. Why not Swiss engineering?"

"Maybe because I'm good. You've heard of good old American know-how?"

"A skill at shutting the eyes to what one doesn't care to see."

"Where the money comes from . . . ? A secret bank account would surprise me very much. Money in secret accounts lies idle. Bankers might consider that—for another man's money. For themselves, idleness is not permitted. Money must be kept hard at it to make more money. Bankers despise lazy money."

I was talking too much and saying too little, and the gendarmes were getting bored with me. It did occur to me that I had something I could tell them with every expectation that they would find it more interesting, but for some not easily accountable reason I found myself unwilling to speak. And they were doing nothing to make me feel cooperative, at least hardly so much that I would want to turn them loose on Mme Douvaine. It was a question of keys to the flat. She had her key and I had mine. She wore hers at her waist, dangling from a huge key ring. Mine, when it was not on a hook just inside the apartment door, would always be in my pocket. It was an accepted fact that there were no others lying about loose, certainly none that might fall into the hands of burglars.

"De Montbard was not a good man. We have been keeping an eye on him."

"Not close enough. That's plain."

"Now we shall be watching you."

"And when you have recovered my garbage, do I get it back?"

"That depends on what we may find in it, M. Erridge. With de Montbard we overlooked garbage. We don't make the same mistake twice."

"I'm glad. It gives me a great feeling."

At a loss for a suitable exit line, they simply left me. My neighbor returned to his own flat. I started on the Herculean job of setting things to rights.

I hadn't gone very far with this before I made an interesting discovery. I came on the doorkey. It dangled from one in a line of clothes hooks on the vestibule wall alongside the door. This discovery stopped me cold.

Usually there was a shirt or some such dangling there, but now there was nothing but the key. The problem, however, was that there was also the key in my pocket, today at least. This demanded an explanation from Mme Douvaine. It was not at all like her to have permitted her key to have gone astray, and this phenomenon of a third key she would have to explain.

I couldn't even for a moment entertain the possibility that she might be working in collaboration with the violators of my landlord's property, but the gendarmes had demonstrated themselves to be powerful conclusion-jumpers; I was prepared to rate them as being of Olympic caliber. I was taking no bets on which way they might be likely to jump this time. Pocketing the key and locking the door behind me, I went in search of Mme Douvaine.

Hers was the last house in the village. It was distinguished from its more impressive neighbors chiefly by virtue of its location. Tucked away between the post office and the churchyard, it alone was removed from the lakefront, and it further concealed itself behind an all but impenetrable curtain of climbing roses. Directly across the road from it was the corner of the castle wall and the entrance to the footpath that skirted the wall.

Crossing the tiny patch of front garden, I had only one thing on my mind and that was how I was to manage getting into the house. It was by no means such a stronghold as its larger neighbors, but it lacked nothing of their fourteenth-century seclusiveness. Its windows were narrow slits cut in the thick stone walls. They would offer no mode of access. There lay nothing here but inhospitality. I could only hope for an open door. Why I should have imagined Mme Douvaine to be showing little concern about the crime wave and why I had no expectation of finding her in a condition that might enable her to respond to a knock at her door, I shall never know. I did, however, have such expectation.

I knocked and it was as I had feared. There was no response to my knock.

Familiar as I was with the high regard in which

Mme Douvaine held locks, I had no reason to hope that on this one occasion she might have convenienced me with a touch of carelessness. Nevertheless, I did try the door, and slowly it swung inward. Prevailing easily over the scent of the roses, the characteristic air of Mme Douvaine's kitchen took over. It wasn't the garlic alone, however, for there was an unmistakably sinister admixture, something sharply acrid.

My hand found the light switch just inside the door. Mme Douvaine was also just inside the door.

She was lying prone on her polished floor tiles and she was sleeping soundly. Her nose and mouth were covered, but the covering was more like a poultice than a gag. It lay loosely across the lower part of her face. It was a cloth soaked in chloroform. Mme Douvaine was zonked.

I removed the rag and tossed it aside. Her breathing seemed to be regular, neither rapid nor sluggish, and there was nothing labored about it. The pinkish hairs of her sparse mustache rose and fell in steady rhythm. I picked her up off the floor and carried her to her bed.

Any attempt to rouse her was clearly beyond my powers. I toyed with the idea of undressing her so that she might sleep more comfortably, but confronted with the impenetrable mysteries of her multifarious hooks and fasteners, I backed away from any such project. I'm a man who knows when he's licked.

My next thought was another call to the police, but I could see little hope of that accomplishing anything much. I backed away from that one as well.

CHAPTER 3

Locking her door behind me, I left her to her rest. Any thought of questioning her could wait until morning. Meanwhile, I needed dinner.

The cafés in town were not inviting. Granted that they commanded magnificent views of the lake, but those I could have from my own terrace, and my freezer held the better dinner Mme Douvaine had cooked for me. I hit the road and headed down to Talloires, where on the shores of Lake Annecy Le Père Bise would do me a great meal. Every night in his lakeside restaurant the old man earned his Michelin three stars anew.

There's no point in being tantalizing with any detailed rundown on the great way he fed me. We can just leave it that I took the road back to Lake Geneva well content. But back in the flat I was confronted with a fresh surprise: I found my bed occupied.

The occupant was the breathtakingly beautiful Mathilde de Montbard. How she came there was a mystery that defied solution. All known keys had been accounted for, so unless she had somehow found yet another key, there was no explaining it.

I left that for thinking about later. Erridge is not a man who will look a gift filly in the mouth, particularly since the lady confronted me with none of those mysterious hooks or fasteners that might have been beyond my coping. I stripped down and climbed into bed beside her. Again I shan't tantalize with any detailed account. Let it suffice that I consoled myself well with everything that happened next.

Morning brought the most extraordinary development. It was breakfast in bed, served to us by a de Montbard manservant. I thought I had been doing well, but I had never achieved such croissant or such butter, such jam or such coffee. The de Montbards were well cared for. And that breakfast was by no means the whole of the joys of the occasion. It occurred to me that I could expect a very considerable rise in my stock with the gendarmes. They had, after all, been much concerned about my sex life or possibly by the lack thereof.

We were still in bed when Mme Douvaine arrived to do up the flat. It was hardly an opportune moment for putting questions to her. To my astonishment, she was not in the least perturbed beyond the fact that the place was by no means in any such state of neatness as her standards demanded. It just wasn't in proper shape for the entertainment of guests. If she thought that its chaos was a product of our nighttime diversions, she was giving no indication of it. She was completely preoccupied with neating up. That I might have offered the lady entertainments that had diminished her sensitivity to disorder mattered not at all to Mme Douvaine. It was her honor that had suffered damage.

Mme de Montbard was, meanwhile, evidencing a great interest in my garbage. She found its loss a matter of profound significance and was insatiable in her curiosity about what it might have contained. I did my best and, with Mme Douvaine's assistance, I did very well; but it was not good enough. The widow could work up no interest in what we had been eating during the week, and it was her opinion that the burglars would have been equally dissatisfied with such a catalogue.

"The savages wanted money, nothing but money," she said. "Stale lettuce would have been of no interest to them."

"Sorry," I said. "No money. Is that what went out in your garbage?"

"It was not my garbage. It was Henri-Edouard's."

"My apologies."

"You don't know the location of the garbage dump?"

"It has never been a matter of interest to me."

"Men! They have no interest in useful knowledge."

"I never expected it would be useful."

"You should have done."

"So now I am interested. Where is the dump?"

"Across the lake in Switzerland, of course. Where else would garbage be?"

"If it's a secret garbage dump, how could I have known?"

"Henri-Edouard knew."

"Henri-Edouard was a practical man."

"Since you are not a practical man, what do you do for money?"

"I work for it. I earn it."

"Yes, of course. That isn't practical. I should have known. After all, you are an American. Americans are romantic about money."

"Engineering is scarcely what I could call romantic."

"Then what else could it be? It's hard-bodied, exotic men in exotic places."

"Nothing so exotic as garbage, Mme de Montbard."

"Garbage is not romantic."

"Not even when it has money in it?"

"There you have a point."

"Unless the dump is a secret one. Anything that is secret is necessarily romantic."

"Would you like to have your pistol back?"

"It isn't a pistol. It's a revolver."

"Pistol or revolver. How should I know? I am just an innocent little woman."

"Permit me to doubt that."

"You are being ungallant."

"Sorry. Since you are offering, I would like the revolver back."

"Come to me tonight and I will have it for you."

"In your bed?"

"My bed or your bed. It will be your preference."

"How do you come to have it?"

"Let it suffice that I do have it."

"Why must I wait for tonight?"

"Because you must earn it."

"My revolver and I must earn it. Is that fair?"

"All of life is manifestly unfair. Surely you must know that. Even romantics know that much."

"What about my garbage? When shall I have that back?"

"Are you sure that you want it back?"

"Since it appears to be in demand, yes."

"You will need to go to the dump to find it."

"But first I must know where to find the dump."

"Be a good boy and I shall take you."

"Today?"

"You are oddly impatient for it."

"Oddly enough, it interests me."

"Even if there's no money in it?"

"There's no money in it."

"Then we'll be wasting our time."

"Isn't that what time is for—to be wasted?"

It was an extraordinary journey. It was well that the Porsche is fitted with bucket seats. Otherwise I should have been hard put to keep Mathilde de Montbard off my lap. Not that I would have much wanted to.

Out at the garbage dump we found the ground shaggy with Swiss fuzz, running barefoot through the garbage. Mme de Montbard couldn't have been more avid in her search for my refuse, and the cops joined her in her avidity. She was in no way averse to befouling her diamonds with the filth, but that could have been because they had been dirtily acquired.

As I expected, our search turned up nothing but my stale lettuce leaves and they left the police as bored as Mathilde had predicted they would be.

We pulled away from the dump and on the way back around the lake we broke for lunch. For that, it was Lausanne and the highly touted establishment of M. Crissier. He has been hailed as the world's greatest chef and I suppose that for Switzerland he might just do, but not to be forgotten was that not too far away across the border Le Père Bise was practicing his magic. Even the Swiss, corrupted as they may have been by Calvin, should have been making the journey.

Over lunch the lady waxed autobiographical. Even though I had questions that clamored for the asking, I went along, listening to the lady's autobiography. It was a good choice: she enjoyed talking about herself and she covered the ground exhaustively. De Montbard had found her in a questionable Alexandria disco, where she had been a belly dancer. (In Alexandria, of course, all discos are questionable.) This oriental background, of course, could be taken into account for the oriental skills she brought to her amatory practices; even the rupestrian paintings on the walls of the Hindu caves could have taught that baby nothing. The belly-dancing assignment had carried a sideline of rolling drunks. She could speak of it with no trace of bad conscience since, in her opinion, they had been well compensated. "You have them with their clothes off and all the rest follows," she said. I could take it that she had refrained from rolling me since everything she might have wanted from me had already been taken.

Mathilde de Montbard furnished me with a catalogue of her lovers. It was well sprinkled with the names of no few of the most prominent men in Geneva. Her memory for names, places, and modes of lovemaking was phenomenal. It might have been that the diamonds served as a mnemonic aid. She ticked these off, stone by stone. Obviously she had not been averse to fouling them earlier that day, in light of the way she had acquired them. That de Montbard had likewise been straying from the marital bed troubled her not at all. She supplied me with a full list of his conquests, but any names of the garbage collector's relatives were absent from the list. The list of the cuckolded was liberally sprinkled with the names of men of great eminence in the financial circles of Geneva and Zurich, not to speak of governmental circles in Paris.

At length I did ask my questions.

"How do you come to have my doorkey and revolver? How did you come by them?"

"Quite naturally. I rolled the robbers for them."

"And that is natural?"

"Since I had them in my bed, why not?"

"It's your custom to take murderers to your bed?"

"Hardly my custom. When I can, I have my men singly . . . and I also make choices."

"And with the murderers you had no choice?"

"I *prefer* to be more discriminating."

"How many of them were there?"

"Only two."

"Only?"

"When Mathilde de Montbard cannot manage two, she will take herself into a convent."

"You will make an interesting nun."

"I shall be very dull."

"What about de Montbard's women? Did you choose them for him?"

"No. He made his own choices."

"I've been speculating about jealous husbands. That's what they're thinking in Geneva."

"Geneva." The lady was scornful. "Since Henri-Edouard was French, they can think nothing else. It's the Swiss myth."

"Nevertheless, what about jealous husbands? It's a classic among murder motives, isn't it?"

"Possibly, but not for them. They were pussy-cats. Henri-Edouard had all of them bought. They danced to his tune."

"And his murderers didn't?"

"Let's say they grew tired of it."

"Then there *were* jealous husbands."

"He had . . . other tunes as well."

"Then explain his murderers, since you have intimate knowledge of them."

"They are savages. They have no ear for music unless it is the clink of coins, gold coins."

"But that didn't stop your having them in your bed."

"It wasn't for making music."

"There's one thing I cannot understand. You had them in your bed. It is to be assumed that you and they are very close. Can you give me any good reason why they should have stolen my garbage, only to deliver it to the dump?"

"Oh, that's easy. They didn't deliver it immediately. They examined it first."

"Weren't you with them when they were examining it?"

"No, I wasn't. I have little taste for garbage."

"From the way you went at it out at the dump, I would have disputed that."

"The dump was different."

"How different?"

"There I was looking for something."

"For what? They had already examined it. If they had come on anything of value, they would have grabbed it."

"Yes, but they are as stupid as dirt. There could have been important papers they would have missed. After all, why else would you now want it returned?"

"But there weren't any. I was disappointed."

"No more than was I."

"I thought you had no interest in money. You said Henri-Edouard kept you well provided."

"Yes. But whatever he had should now be mine. Can I be wrong in wanting that?"

"Tell me. Did you engineer his murder?"

"I am no engineer. You are."

"That doesn't answer my question."

"I was satisfied with Henri-Edouard. I could have replaced him many times if I had ever thought I could have done better. I liked what he provided."

"I know. He was soft and pillowy."

"Make no mistake, my friend. There can be comfort in that."

"For a loving wife you are extraordinarily cold-blooded."

"Not at all. I was never a loving wife. Henri-Edouard did not expect it. He understood me. You see, he was not a romantic like you."

We left it at that and I took her back to her house. This time I didn't have to call the gendarmes—the lady did it for me. Their promise that they would be keeping an eye on me was all too well borne out. They were appallingly well informed. Nothing of what had passed between Mathilde de Montbard and me was unknown to them, and they minced no words.

CHAPTER 4

"You lost no time, M. Erridge, before you took possession of Henri-Edouard de Montbard's widow."

"Of no more than my share in her, gentlemen."

"Need we tell you that the lady is an Egyptian whore?"

"There can be nothing you might tell me that I have not already had from her."

"With ample demonstration."

"If you say so."

"You require more?"

"No. I was well satisfied."

"Did she tell you when she would be returning your revolver?"

"What makes you think she has it?"

"She has never yet taken a man to her bed and not gotten something for it."

"It would appear that you know the lady well."

"We keep dossiers on all harlots, and her husband was a hoarder of gold."

"Could it have been gold in his garbage?"

"The gold has disappeared. It must be somewhere."

"She seems to think it is. She tells me that everything he had should now be hers. She wants it."

"Enough to have murdered him for it?"

"Allow me to doubt that. She had too many

other available choices. You yourself told me that she had many lovers."

"Your dam was to be Swiss-financed. Was he to have financed it?"

"It's my understanding that he was not Swiss. Was he not French?"

"Only since he has no longer been German. He was the Herr Heinrich von Liedberg until the Weimar Republic took the 'von' out of life in Germany."

For that quip the gendarme had switched into English. I assumed it was with the sole purpose of being able to make it "fun." To him the pun was hilarious. I laughed dutifully.

When they had finished their questioning, I again had my business appointments to keep in Geneva, although I went with little of business on my mind.

Even though Geneva seemed a strange place to go in search of my stolen garbage, it seemed to me that it would be my best bet. I had been too long playing a lone hand in a situation where a man had need of allies. I had friends in Geneva and they were men who exercised very considerable power on both sides of the border. To have relied on Mathilde de Montbard as an ally struck me as being foolhardy.

Before quitting the gendarmes, however, I ventured a few experimental questions.

"How are you doing toward recovering my revolver?" I asked.

"It will be coming back to you tonight. Was that not promised?"

"Are you prepared to rest on that?"

"Madame de Montbard is notoriously reliable."

The adverb appeared to be too well chosen to be accidental.

"And my garbage? What about that?"

"Why are you so eager to have it back, if it is only garbage?"

"It is difficult to believe that it is no more than garbage since it is so much in demand."

"On the garbage have you not also had the lady's promise?"

I pulled out and headed across the border. My friends there were the giants of the Geneva and Zurich financial markets. I consulted with one of them about the garbage problem. He took a dim view of my wish to have it returned to me. I protested.

"Since others are showing so great an interest," I said, "I must be interested as well."

"You will do better if you leave it alone."

"That is probably excellent advice but it is an admonition I must disregard."

"I hope you recognize that you have taken to living dangerously."

"In what respect?"

"Mathilde de Montbard takes many men to her bed."

"Including no few of your colleagues. But with me she did it differently. She took me to my bed."

"Certainly a negligible difference. She has lovers who are less complaisant than Henri-Edouard used to be. They are bloodthirsty men and given to jealousy. It will be your blood they will be hungering for. You must recognize that she accommodated my colleagues *before* she took to consorting with murderers."

"It could be the easiest available way of finding them. They have something from my garbage."

"Your obsession with your garbage, my friend, is hardly useful. I'm telling you that you might be well advised to give it up."

"And the lady?"

"She should be given up as well."

"I would be loath to do that."

"Understandable but unwise. You cannot have fallen into the error of falling in love with the delectable Mathilde de Montbard."

"You recognize that she is delectable."

"Indisputably. Delectable and dangerous. You cannot enjoy being constantly in the eye of the police."

"And theirs is not the only eye. You, too, seem to be all-seeing."

"It is our practice to learn what we need to know."

"Even when it involves prying?"

"You happen to be important to us, Matthew. We make every effort to keep you out of trouble."

"That is kind even though it is annoying."

"You must believe me when I tell you that the lady is trouble."

"And you must believe me when I tell you that she is eminently worth it."

"I wouldn't venture to doubt that, but nonetheless . . ."

This gentleman who appeared to have appointed himself guardian of my safety and good conduct was one Gaspard Lapointe, a genius of international finance and, it was said, of intercontinental intrigue. Of the latter I could scarcely pretend to know. But the fact that he was privy to my bedroom exploits could certainly serve as an indication of the possibility.

I found it difficult to believe that he could have been in the confidence of Mathilde de Montbard, and it was even more difficult to believe it of Mme Douvaine. I'd had ample experience of that lady's devotion to gossip, but I had been flattering myself on being the sole recipient of her gleanings.

Just as I was about ready to give up on the good Gaspard and go seek my intelligence elsewhere, he came up with the most startling suggestion.

"If you are serious about persisting in your effort to recover your garbage," he said, "you will need to go to Paris to seek it out there."

"Paris is a long way for garbage to travel."

"And hardly worth the journey, since you have already inspected it on the garbage dump."

"Quite so, but my interest is not in the garbage

except insofar as it might lead me to the men who stole it."

"Then I recommend Paris. Paris, after all, was de Montbard's base of operations."

"I had been thinking it was Geneva."

"Only in a small way. He valued it mainly for its proximity to the lake, since the lake was convenient to the garbage scow."

"Then it was money in his garbage?"

"Gold, illegally exported out of France. De Montbard was terrified of Mitterand and of the Mitterand laws, which were directed against him and his ilk. These men are milking all their hard currency out of the country and that cannot be permitted to continue. It takes little more to make a government fall—and Mitterand's government, at best, is tottering."

"So the gold was destined for the garbage dump."

"It was to be intercepted en route and taken to a more suitable place, but the wrong people got to it first."

"So the garbage collector was an innocent victim."

"Hardly innocent, since he was trying to play both ends against the middle. He murdered de Montbard and made off with the garbage bags only to be murdered himself, in turn."

"I cannot understand this. What then is all this nonsense that's been coming at me ever since?"

"Mme de Montbard in your bed? We cannot disregard your obvious attractions. Also, however, what was his should now be hers and she wants it. It's that simple."

"No. The theft of my garbage. The ransacking of my flat. What could all that have been? If the killers have the gold, what can they hope to have from me?"

"Ah, but they don't have the gold. Henri-Edouard was not that trusting. All they have for their pains is his garbage. The gold he has stowed away in a safe place, probably buried in his garden."

"That I should call impossible. He was too fat to dig."

"You are probably right. That means it will have to be somewhere in the house if he hasn't contrived to move it over to Switzerland earlier."

"What baffles me," I said, "is all this elaborate contrivance. It could have been done so easily. The Swiss border customs barrier on the highway is totally meaningless. No car is ever stopped, no papers are ever examined, nobody has ever been searched."

"True enough for you and me, my friend, but not for Henri-Edouard. The gendarmes had been alerted by Paris. Such great quantities of money cannot be transported without its becoming known. The police were watching him. A border crossing for him meant a body search every time and he knew it. He was certainly noisy enough about it here in Geneva. He kept asking if the stu-

pid gendarmes could possibly believe that he was
carrying his gold concealed up his ass."

I abandoned Gaspard and tried a few of the other
gentlemen. I was hitting upon characters Mathilde
de Montbard had included in her catalogue of
bedfellows. They seemed less well informed than
Gaspard, but that could have been because they
were gentlemen and had an interest in preserving
the secrecy of their dealings with the lovely Mathilde. They were André Gallatin, Hilaire Talbot,
and Bernard McMahon. And they were unanimous
in advising me to forget my garbage. None of
them, however, suggested that I give up Mathilde.
It was their universal opinion that she was em-
barked on a husband hunt and that I was the leading contender.

"You are a civilized man, mon ami. She cannot
but prefer you to the animals who freed her of the
pig. Also she brings a substantial dowry with her. I
know that you Americans are contemptuous of
such things, but they are not to be disregarded."

The suggestion that I give serious thought to the
dowry came from good old Hilaire. It was his mis-
fortune that he already had a wife. The man was
drooling with desire for it.

Driving back across the line, I was thinking
about the trip up to Paris. I had no appetite for it.
Don't get me wrong—I have nothing against Paris.
It has always been one of my favorite playpens. But
I would need to devote my days to hanging around

the Bourse, and that's not a neighborhood where a guy is going to find himself playmates. I began thinking that I had been blowing this thing up out of all proper proportion.

True enough, two men had been killed. Their murderers had been playing games with my garbage, and what with killers and Mathilde making free with my place, I could hardly call my home my castle—all that thick masonry to the contrary notwithstanding. But the time had come, I was thinking, for me just to let the whole thing go. I'd been promised the return of my revolver, and I had no need of my garbage. If I simply ignored it, all the nonsense would simply go away.

That I might have been influenced by the suggestion that I held the inside track with the beautiful and talented Mathilde de Montbard I cannot deny. A man would need to be a clod to walk away from that, even if he wasn't drooling for her magnificent dowry. I couldn't help thinking that the lady was possessed of talents she had still to reveal to me. Mathilde was an education and I was certainly not too old to learn.

I still had my peace to make with Mme Douvaine. I called at the lady's house and there I was accorded the frostiest of receptions. She was unable to understand why I should now be coming to bother her. I was inclined to think that she would not have received me at all, if she hadn't been afflicted with a great curiosity that she was compelled to satisfy. There was gossip to be had and Mme Douvaine was not to be denied.

"Mme de Montbard is not a good woman," she said, smacking her lips.

"That must be a matter of opinion."

"There was much enjoyment for you, was there not?"

"There was and I must thank you for providing it."

"Thank me? But you are making the mistake, monsieur."

"It must have been you who admitted her to the flat."

"When I was lying on my bed like the dead? No, M. Erridge. You must know that the lady is a witch. For the devil there are no locks, and it was the devil who admitted her to your flat."

"I don't believe in the devil."

"If you will lie with witches, you had better believe in him."

Mme Douvaine had the whole thing figured out: she had herself been the victim of witchcraft. She could accept no other explanation for her unconsciousness. The disorder she had found in the flat she was assuming had been of Mathilde de Montbard's doing: she had been looking for her husband's gold. It appeared to be common knowledge that it was gold that had gone astray in the de Montbard garbage.

"What makes you think it was gold?" I asked.

She countered question with question. "What else would men murder for?"

"With such a witch for a wife there might also be jealousy."

"There is no jealousy when every man can have her."

"When may I expect to have the flat to myself again? I am tired of being invaded."

"You must leave that to me, M. Erridge. I can fix it so that you won't be troubled any more."

I asked her how she proposed to do that.

"I shall hang a crucifix on your door. No devil can go past a cross."

"And I shall then have no more visits from Mme de Montbard?"

"You will find her in her own bed. She will be waiting for you."

"How can you know that?"

"You are a man that women wait for."

"Even witches?"

"Especially witches."

I asked her if she might reconsider her decision to leave my employ. She was clearly torn, but the opportunity of displaying her prowess against the Powers of Darkness was more than the good woman could resist. I expected that she might try to exact from me a promise of future good behavior, but she attempted nothing so stringent.

I went home and took my drinks and my dinner out on the terrace. I noticed that there were lights next door in the de Montbard manse. Inexplicably the whole house was ablaze with light. It streamed out of every window. If the lady was waiting for me as she had indicated she would be, and as Mme Douvaine assured me she would be, it seemed most unlikely that she should have encumbered herself with a house full of company, but I could think of no other satisfactory explanation for all the lights. I finished my dinner and carted the dishes back inside. After loading the dishwasher and starting it going, I returned to the terrace, where I relaxed with a cognac.

It occurred to me that the police might have released de Montbard's body to his widow and that Geneva had come over in full force to view the remains. I locked up and took myself next door either to join the crowd of mourners or to continue my education. With Mathilde de Montbard, of course, there was no need for it to be either/or. It could easily be both.

I walked into an empty house. If my place had been chaotic the day before, the de Montbard house was now a monument of disorder. Everything had been turned inside out, and in a house that far outdid my flat in its accoutrements, the stuff lay about not in heaps but in mountains.

I had not been there before, but exploration wasn't difficult. The layout was conventional and it was easy to locate the master bedroom.

Even before I was in the room, I smelled the gunpowder. For a moment I was struck with the absurd thought that Mme Douvaine would have identified it as brimstone, the scent of witchcraft. I put that thought aside and replaced it with the certainty of gunfire. The bedroom, like the rest of the house, was chaotic but, unlike the rest of the house, this was bloodstained chaos. Half buried in a great pile of dresses and scarves and slacks I found Mathilde de Montbard. She was dead.

Since she was stark naked, the wounds were easily located. They were all too like those of her late husband. Again they were three—one in the head, one in the heart, and one in the beautiful round belly. Alongside the body lay my revolver. It had been fired. Four chambers were empty. Counting the one a prudent man keeps empty, they had cradled the three slugs that had taken her life. Her killer had been a prudent man.

CHAPTER 5

It was a time when I should have been doing some serious thinking, but I made the error of acting first. If I had permitted myself the delusion that I was involved in an affair where my involvement was at the least open to question, I was now confronted with a situation that was fundamentally changed. It was no longer any trivial matter of purloined garbage. It was three people murdered and one of the three the beautiful Mathilde de Montbard. Nobody could expect that I should ignore that, certainly not after the lady had been so generous in granting me her favors.

When I should have been on the telephone putting a call through to the gendarmes, I was giving them not even the first thought. Instead I made the great mistake of taking off for Paris. I didn't make it. On the autoroute just outside Dijon the gendarmes flagged me down. If previously I had been suspect, they had now been snowed under by a mountain of evidence. The lady had been dispatched with slugs fired out of my revolver. The ballistics lads had come up with test results that indicated that both the garbage collector and de Montbard had been eliminated by the same means. Now far more than the de Montbard gold was missing. Mathilde de Montbard's diamonds had also been stolen.

In the opinion of the gendarmes the diamonds might well have represented a fortune at least the equal of the gold. It was no secret that the lady had been expecting me that night and they had Mme Douvaine's testimony to the effect that I had been headed in that direction. There were also various neighbors who had seen me enter the de Montbard house. It seemed to me that such a plethora of evidence should have served toward establishing my innocence—surely no guilty man would have pointed so many fingers at himself. But then again I had stupidly compounded suspicion by taking flight. That I had taken it in the least useful direction appeared to count for nothing. The road into Switzerland or through the Mont Blanc tunnel down into Italy would have been far easier for me than the long pull up to Paris, but it was assumed that I had been counting on my influential friends and my American passport. My friends did rally round, but there was no way that their influence could stretch to encompass aid to a suspected murderer.

The *Guide Michelin* warmly recommends Dijon for sightseeing and for gastronomy. Although the Palais de Justice does appear on the sightseeing list, it is its ceilings *Michelin* goes for and those are not in the section given over to the pokey. If that region could have been considered remarkable for anything, it would necessarily have been for the rats. In the same way, the gastronomic delights of *cuisine dijonnais* were unknown in those quarters. They were a far cry from the Chapeau Rouge.

I was, furthermore, in a country that operated under the Code Napoléon. In other words, I was presumed to be guilty until proved innocent, and proof of innocence doesn't come easily when a man has been stupid. Not having Mathilde de Montbard's diamonds might have been a point in my favor. Baby and I were both subjected to a body search, and I began to comprehend the justice of Henri-Edouard's complaint.

The revolver, of course, was the chief piece of evidence against me. I had at least had the wit to leave it where it lay, although I had, however briefly, been silly enough to contemplate pocketing it. Mathilde de Montbard had, after all, promised that I would have it back if I came to her. I was inclined to the belief that the odd way she had chosen to return it made no material difference, but good sense quickly told me that it made a vast difference. Had it not, in fact, come back unearned?

What finally came to weigh in my favor and persuaded the magistrates of my innocence I could not then know, but the time came when I was released and allowed to resume my journey up to Paris. Although I was released from custody, I was by no means freed from suspicion. That clung to me and I was kept under close surveillance.

In Paris I learned the reason why I had regained my freedom. Mathilde de Montbard's diamonds had been of virtually no value. They had been paste. It had not been gold that Henri-Edouard, in his terror of Mitterand's socialism, had spirited out of France. He had, in manifold transactions, converted his surplus wealth into diamonds. As he had acquired the stones, he had arranged to have them duplicated in paste across the border in Switzerland. In the course of several trips across the line, Mathilde had worn the gems into Switzerland and had returned identically bedecked but in paste replicas. I was indebted to the diamond dealers of the Place Vendôme and the Rue de la Paix for this intelligence. Obviously Mathilde had been her husband's collaborator in this deception. At least she had been cooperating with him until it suited her purposes to have the fat man blown away.

The garbage bag nonsense had been nothing more than a charade designed to deceive the gendarmes. Since the transfer had already been accomplished, this had only been a touch of bombast and it had cost de Montbard dearly. But since the beautiful Mathilde had from the first been a party to the deception, her behavior subsequent to Henri-Edouard's murder now became inexplicable.

In Paris I made no inquiries about my garbage. My situation was far too grave for that. I was on a hunt now for killers, and even though I was advised to leave that to the police, I was not disposed to do so. That seemed like taking the easy route, and I could not put it out of my head that the easy way would be the craven and shameful way. Honor demanded it of me that I do something; and, being under suspicion, I could hardly afford to sit idle.

"This is not America, mon ami. Our gendarmes here have no patience with vigilantes. They prefer to do their own work. In the provinces they may be lazy but here in Paris under the eyes of the Ministry they are not."

"That is all very well, but it happens that they are working on me—and that I don't like."

"Give them time. They will learn better."

"But I have no time. The killers act quickly. I cannot expect that they will give me time. Not so long as they hold my revolver. Those buckos are itchy-fingered."

"Nevertheless, you will be well advised to leave them alone."

I was having this counsel from an old friend, Albert Rigaud. Albert was a fellow engineer. We had worked a couple of jobs together, and he would be joining me soon on the dam project. I knew his toughness and I knew his good heart. He recommended that I find myself a girl.

It would need to be an experienced girl, he said, who could explore for me those erogenous zones Mathilde de Montbard had not yet reached before her untimely death. I doubted that there could be any such. It was my feeling that Mathilde had neglected nothing, but it was Albert's contention that I was underestimating myself. I appreciated his solicitude but felt that I was not yet ready. That this made him wonder whether I mightn't be suffering a diminishing manhood was regrettable. I tried to make him understand that my stay in jail had temporarily arrested my carnal appetites. He was under the impression that incarceration greatly increased a man's hunger, but he had never been jailed in Dijon; he offered a fervent prayer that the condition might be no more than temporary: it would be a great pity for so powerful a performer to have been lost to the arena of love.

Albert, one must appreciate, was incorrigibly French. No man has ever been more completely free of envy. He was all admiration. For him potency was all.

It might be thought that in Paris I would be free of any of those annoyances that had been afflicting me in my Savoyard hideaway. I surely had come far enough, and the killers had had ample opportunity to learn that with me they could only come up empty. Even their attempt to divert suspicion from themselves by directing it toward me was falling on its face. The time should now have come for them to turn their ugly attentions elsewhere. Those guys, however, were inexhaustible.

The concierge in the hotel that has always been my favorite Paris stamping ground is an old pal, in every respect the traveling boy's best friend. The maids compete at mothering me, and there is not a Mme Douvaine among them. The valet de chambre I have known since his infancy. It is the last place in the world where one could look for treachery.

Even there, however, I was invaded. My hotel

room was ransacked. The killers seemed to be making a habit of it, although there was nothing there for them to find and by then they should have known it. The pickings would have been even slimmer than back in the flat. But there it was. Somebody had penetrated the impenetrable.

It couldn't have been anyone on the hotel staff. I was ready to trust them with my life and there was no possibility of any breach of that trust.

The whole hotel went into a frenzy. This was shameful and it was unprecedented. No one could explain it. Everyone was desolate. The concierge searched his records and finally came up with something. Shortly after my arrival, two men had checked in and had been assigned to a room adjacent to mine. They were patrons new to the hotel. All the other residents were old-timers, people who had been coming there year after year. Only the two newcomers could be suspect. The concierge was prepared to do a search of their room for the recovery of my stolen property. He was also bent on calling in the gendarmes.

I vetoed the search, explaining that it could only be unproductive since I was missing nothing. In Savoy it had been only my garbage, but here there was not even that.

"No underpants, monsieur? Here in France American underwear is much coveted."

"You forget that I checked in without luggage. My departure from Savoy was hurried."

"Not even so much as a handkerchief?"

"Not even a tissue."

"Unfortunate, monsieur, most unfortunate. It leaves us powerless to act. Worse that that, it leaves the gendarmes powerless. No crime has been committed."

"What about trespassing?" I asked.

"A small crime, but it might do."

He was reaching for the phone. I stopped him.

"I'd prefer you'd leave the gendarmes out of this," I said, quickly regretting having brought up trespassing.

"They do not like to be left out. It does a hotel no good."

"Having them in does a hotel less good."

"We cannot allow that to be a consideration."

"I have been looking for these two men. It may well be that I have now found them."

"You cannot want to consort with them. They are bad men."

The concierge has always been concerned for my morality and, Paris being what it is, his concern has not been without reason.

"They have been hunting me. The time has come when I should begin hunting them."

"That can be dangerous, monsieur."

"Yes. Hunting is a dangerous sport."

Since it was now obvious that the two strangers in the next room were my two killers, I set myself to tail them.

Paris may be the City of Light. Lights, after all,

are one of the many attractions for which it is famous. But it has its dark places, and the chase that
night took me into most of them. There is the standard tourist route: the Place Pigalle, the Quartier
Latin, the Grands Boulevards, Montmartre. That
precious pair shunned all of those. Where they
went, I followed, and they took me into the area
around the Gare de l'Est.

This quarter is little known. It's the stamping
ground of the Algerians and of the *pieds noirs*. The
air is laden with the reek of couscous and hashish,
and the area bristles with little *boîtes* enlivened by
belly dancers. If Mathilde had not acquired Henri-
Edouard in Alexandria, this would have been her
next port of call. On my own I would have eschewed any such questionable delights as these, but
I was not on my own. My two friends were hitting
all the hot spots. It may have been with the purpose of plucking the diamond out of some belly
dancer's navel, but if that was their intention they
were making no moves. They were models of propriety, just two innocent boys hungering for seduction. It was a long night, but I stayed with them
even after I'd become convinced they were having
themselves a night off. It was possible, of course,
that they knew they were being followed and were
giving me an eyeful in an effort to convince me that
I was barking up the wrong tree. But I was certain
that I had been most skillful in my pursuit and that
they could not possibly suspect.

I persisted, and the next day I tried again. This

time, however, it was not any of the dark places. Obviously dressed and groomed for the occasion, they hit the posh jewelers in the Place Vendôme and along the Rue de la Paix. The diamond dealers were a smooth lot, suave and slick. If they had any suspicion that they might be entertaining customers more given to robbery than to purchase, they offered no indication of it. They might have been dealing with Henri-Edouard de Montbard.

It was in one of the jeweler's shops that I ran into Albert, who insisted on carting me off for lunch. I was not so easily diverted, but when he said he had important news for me, that did it.

He took me to Archestrate and fed me all too well. After a lunch like that, a man is good for nothing but an afternoon nap. But his news was startling. In fact, it was the talk of Paris. I hadn't heard it because word had not come to the Gare de l'Est, even though it would have been of great interest there. The de Montbard diamonds had come back onto the market and they were being scooped up by none other than my good buddy Gaspard.

"So he has a mistress and he's doing her well," I said.

"You must be joking. You don't know that Gaspard is gay?"

"I've seen indications."

"Has he never made a play for you? He makes a specialty of tough Americans."

"Then I may not have been tough enough for him."

"Mathilde de Montbard gave you good marks, my friend."

"Then if I am to learn anything, I'm to go back to Geneva?"

"If you care to risk it."

"What's the risk?"

"Gaspard. He is a powerful man. He could be a bad enemy."

"I can handle Gaspard Lapointe."

"Don't be too sure. He has much influence, far too much."

"We have always been friends."

"I wouldn't count on it."

I had my nap and then I gave myself a second night of shadowing my neighbors. This time they offered every appearance of being about to oblige me by getting down to business. It was only small business, nothing ambitious. They were out only for maintenance money, just something to go along on, what they thought they might need for meeting day-to-day running expenses. They went after it in the Métro. I thought that would necessarily make it a short night, since the Métro is not like the New York subway: it shuts down at midnight.

The operation was as simple as it was crude. The two of them would flank a man, crowd him close, dive into his pockets, and, removing his billfold, leave the train at the next station. My gendarmes, of course, were witnessing the whole procedure. I could see that they were drooling with eagerness to intervene, but Erridge was their quarry, and they couldn't be pulled off into side issues.

When it came closing time on the Métro, however, the larcenous lads were not ready to call it a night. They switched to the railway stations, specifically the Gare St-Lazare. Passengers, disembarking sleepily from late trains, were easy prey, and guys in the men's room with their flies undone, or even better with their pants down, were much easier.

I wondered how long it would be before they became aware of me. I fully expected that the time would come when they would turn on me and go for my pockets, but I was unable to decide what to do when it happened. I was confident of my ability to fight them off and was curious to see whether in that contingency the gendarmes would go on in their role of cool observers. The two buckos, however, didn't oblige. We returned to the hotel and I went to bed. I was a disappointment to the concierge. I had been allowing my police escort to go to waste.

In the morning I headed back down to Geneva and the lake. It was time for going to the mat with old Gaspard. He had been running free far too long.

I could have been conclusion-jumping when I assumed he might have masterminded the de Montbard murders. Certainly he was possessed of the power that should have permitted him a far subtler approach. Also, it had been Gaspard who had steered me toward Paris.

I could see two ways of viewing that. It could be taken as an indication of his innocence—he had merely been helpful. At least as possible, however, was that it had been his intention to remove me from his theater of operations. A large factor in favor of the innocence hypothesis was Gaspard's access to intelligence. The garbage ploy should never for a moment have misled him. He was too well equipped in sources from which he could be furnished with detailed accountings of the movements of any large sums of money or sizable accumulations of valuables.

Always having avoided Switzerland as much as possible, I didn't know Geneva as well as Paris. I assumed that, like any other large city, it would have its darker side, but I had never had occasion to familiarize myself with it. I now tried to find myself some guidance, but neither Gaspard nor Hilaire was of any assistance—whether through ignorance or unwillingness, I was unable to determine. I tossed some tentative queries in Mme Douvaine's direction but all I got from her were declarations of her unimpeachable virtue. She was a good woman and it was not at all to her liking that I seemed intent on seeking out bad company. Retribution was both certain and savage; the fate of Mathilde de Montbard should be a lesson to me; a man who insisted upon consorting with witches was most certainly courting damnation.

My buddy the postmaster should have been a better bet. He appeared to be a salty character. If *his* information wasn't firsthand, it would be because throughout the years all that telephone eavesdropping had been done in vain. Apart, however, from verifying that Geneva did have its areas and adding that Lausanne, if anything, had even more, the sowing grounds for his wild oats appeared to be Annemasse, and that was of little use to me. Beyond that he left me with the suggestion that the other side of the Mont Blanc tunnel might well hold what I wanted; for imaginative vice he recommended Italy. That, however, was information I didn't need from him.

Although I hadn't intended it, my return to the lake was perfectly opportune for attendance at the de Montbard obsequies. It was a double funeral and a monument of *pompe funèbre*. Everyone and his uncle were there and the flowers were spectacular. The eulogies were such masterpieces of hypocrisy as might well have been written by Molière. That the Swiss didn't laugh was only to have been expected: there is, after all, no race more sober than they. There was, however, not so much as even the first French snicker. It was great theater and thoroughly appreciated as such.

Much to the forefront of the mourners were the pair of killers. They had dressed for the occasion by hauling on the threads they had worn in the Paris jewelers' shops. I could appreciate their need to mourn: they had expended so much effort, and all to no avail. Gaspard, of course, was present, and although I watched for any exchange of signals between him and the murderers, I could see none. They might have been crude operators, but Gaspard was far too slick. He was not going to be caught out that easily. What he did betray was his awareness that I was watching him, and that I had not expected. It seemed at least odd that he should know I might have any reason for suspicion.

I joined the cortège to the cemetery and was duly impressed with the de Montbard tomb. It recalled Mathilde's Egyptian background, although the tombs of the Pharaohs pay far feebler tribute to death. If I had not known that the diamonds were being acquired by Gaspard, I should have thought they might be buried there.

After the burial Gaspard took me to lunch. It was a big party, and for it he had assembled all of the lovely Mathilde's bedfellows. The choice of luncheon guests could not have been other than deliberate; it almost led me to suspect Gaspard of something like wit. But I reminded myself that Gaspard was Swiss and that the Swiss are lacking in humor. Among the patrons of the restaurant were the two killers. I had been loath to accept Gaspard's invitation—I hadn't wanted to lose contact with my two bully boys. So it was a delightful surprise to have them accommodate me by turning up for lunch. I mentioned the two thugs to Gaspard, but it got me nothing. He agreed that they were strange patrons for such an elegant establishment, but that was merely recognition of the obvious. If there was any other recognition, it went without acknowledgment.

Considering the company, it was astonishing that the luncheon went off uneventfully. My guess was that Gaspard was attempting a bit of fishing, and he was undoubtedly disappointed to come away empty-handed.

After lunch I tailed the killers. They were feeding well on their take from the night in the Métro, but it was evident that they were economizing on their lodgings. They led me into an area well back from the lake filled with garages, sex shops, and brothels. They ran to earth in a back-street hotel, not readily distinguishable from one of the brothels. With only the most passing moment of wistfulness as I thought of my flat beside the lake, I followed them in and took a room.

If you subscribe to the delusion that no hotel under Swiss management can be dirty, I recommend a night in the Hôtel du Grand Alp. It has been reported to me since that the management is Bulgarian, but I doubt that. Happily, the furnishings included one small chair made of plastic and innocent of any cracks or crevices that might harbor vermin. The bed was to be shunned. It belonged to the bedbugs and the lice.

But I soon discovered that I'd been hit with the greatest luck. I had been given a room next door to the double that housed my two friends. To make the situation even better the walls were thin, no more than thick enough to provide crawling room for the roaches, and at that they were crowded. I became aware of my neighbors through recognition of their voices. They couldn't have been heard more plainly. It was as if the three of us were sharing a room.

Their conversation was enlightening. If it did nothing else, it expanded my vocabulary. They were talking about good old Gaspard, and the epithets they were loading on him would have curled your hair if only you could have fully understood them. He had "used" them and he had left them poorly paid. (This was a facet of the Gaspard character I would never have suspected.) He had got the diamonds and had fobbed them off with almost nothing. They'd been torn between enticements, whether they were to cut his throat or castrate him; they seemed to find both courses of action equally appealing.

In time their talk turned to me. I had been a disappointment to them. Of course, they should have known better. It had been Gaspard who had put them onto me and they had known from the first that he was not to be trusted. For all the trouble they had taken with me, they'd come up with nothing—not in my garbage and not in my apartment.

CHAPTER 6

I waited out their nap time in my plastic chair. When they woke, they dressed and went out. At a discreet distance I followed. The streets in the district were jammed with men, lined up at the sex shops and the brothels, and it was easy to keep a screen of people between me and my quarries.

At first, however, they were disappointing. Moving only as far as the street corner, they lounged against a light stanchion and watched the passing scene. They could have been a pair of gaping tourists. They were looking in every direction but mine. Whether this avoidance was deliberate or not I did not know, but I was inclined to believe that it wasn't. I was just too well screened from their gaze.

In time they were joined by a third man. As shabbily dressed as they were, he blended nicely into the scene. For a few minutes he lounged with them, but then the three moved on. They didn't go far, only to one of the sex shops a few doors away. There they bent to three coin-in-the-slot peep shows.

The third man I'd been finding troubling. His face was discomfitingly familiar, but still I couldn't get him pinned down. He looked as if he might be French, but he might just as easily have been Swiss. Swiss and French all too often look alike. It was only when he was bent to his peep show that I was able to zero in on him. Dangling from his back pocket were a pair of handcuffs. His being in mufti had deceived me—I had never seen him out of uniform before. This was the head man, Arnin, who had taken charge of my interrogations.

When they pulled out of the sex shop I was on their tail. As they moved down toward the lake, away from the neighborhood of the Grand Alp, the crowds grew thinner. Accordingly, I was forced to follow more carefully. I might even have lost them if I'd not had a good idea of where they were headed. They skirted the grounds of the Palais des Nations and passed a cemetery. They were making a beeline for Gaspard Lapointe's lakeside mansion. I had been there to several parties, so I knew that it was not less palatial than the Palais. The grounds were surrounded by a tall wrought-iron fence and patrolled by a pair of guard dogs. A burly security guard was at the gate, armed with a shotgun, and it was evident that he was not out after birds.

The three guys were discussing what they had in mind for Lapointe. The gendarme recoiled in horror from the first mention of castration. By both nature and training gendarmes are a conservative lot. He took more kindly to the possibility of murder, but he urged that they not hurry it. They were kicking around the question of how they were to get by the dogs and the armed guard, and the gendarme took the guard as his province. "That one," he said, "will be easy. All I'll need to do is show him my badge. The Swiss have a great awe of authority. They are like the Germans. I'll have him rolling over and playing dead."

The two goons decided that poisoned meat would be the best idea for the dogs. Although they were under the impression that dogs had a preference for beef, since this pair belonged to Gaspard they thought that they might need veal, milk-fed veal.

Finally, they started back toward the hotel. On the way, they replenished their income by rolling some drunks they happened to pass. The gendarme merely watched; he neither lent a hand nor intervened. He was only to get a third of the take. I assumed that was for providing such police protection as the company of a French cop in Switzerland might afford. In the middle of town he broke away to go back across the line.

I had no wish to spend a night in the plastic chair at the Grand Alp, so I picked Baby out of the parking lot where I'd stowed her before the funeral. The next night I returned to the Grand Alp, planning a second evening of trailing the two killers.

Again they joined up with the gendarme, but before that they had discussed their displeasure with him: they blamed him for the mistake they had made in going after the garbage. It was, it seems, the gendarme who had put them onto that, and they were of the opinion that he should have known better. Furthermore, they resented the three-way split—they were doing all the dirty work and he was taking his share and doing nothing. On the main event it had been a four-way split, ever since the gendarme had brought Gaspard into the act. Since they were planning to eliminate Gaspard they would be putting an end to that, but meanwhile they felt it was high time that both Gaspard and the gendarme got in there and dirtied their hands, or they would share nothing with them. Tipping them off to the opportunities was not enough, especially because their tips had been going sour.

They informed the gendarme of their decision. Although he protested, he found he didn't have a leg to stand on. Again they moved out of the neighborhood and made it a night of muggings and rolling drunks. Around the perimeter of the Palais des Nations the haul was particularly good. They were hitting drunken diplomats, whom they found to be easy and rich pickings. After the final curtain at the ballet, in the Grand Theâtre, they worked the area around the building; the balletomanes were an incautious lot and they did very well with them. But Geneva is an early-to-bed town, and the crowds soon thinned out. The three divided up the loot and headed home to the Grand Alp.

I followed. I was curious to know whether the gendarme was really prepared to brave the bedbugs and the lice. Since he had been moving about for two nights in close proximity to the two thugs, it could be assumed that the lice had already made the jump. But there were also the bedbugs. To satisfy my curiosity, I followed along and repaired to my plastic chair. They did make a threesome of it.

I drove home to my flat.

In the morning I paid a call on Hilaire. It seemed to me that the time had arrived to make my first move against Gaspard. I would hit the cabal where it was the most vulnerable—in the person of the gendarme. There were many charges that could now be brought against him.

Hilaire's delight at the prospect was too much infected with terror, however: Gaspard was a mighty man, and Hilaire was afraid of him.

"You agree that he must be brought down," I said. "You should be doing it, Hilaire."

"It's impossible, Matthew. He's too powerful."

"He has the diamonds. How did he get them?"

"Out of a safe deposit box."

"Is that possible?"

"For Gaspard everything is possible. He just pays a bribe."

"But then nobody is safe."

"I know. All of us here in Geneva know. It is worrying everybody, and that is not the worst of it. Think of what it means to the reputation of Swiss banking. The financial health of our economy depends on the reputation of Swiss security."

"You need only make things known. You have friends. If all the Geneva bankers act together
. . ."

"He will turn to Zurich. The men of Zurich are his, solidly, all of them."

"I have friends in Zurich. I don't believe it of them. Even if this is so, I can turn them around. I know I can."

"These friends? Are they to be trusted?"

"They're Swiss."

"Gaspard is also Swiss."

"But he is also an embezzler."

"I hope you can bring it off. I wish you luck."

Returning to the lake, I went into a huddle with my neighbor, Georges Bardelot. He was horrified by what I told him of Gaspard's activities. He trembled for the safety of his box at the bank, with his life's savings. And, having no exalted financial position that might be destroyed, he could be with me in making the try at the destruction of Gaspard Lapointe. He agreed to bring the charges against the gendarme. Erridge would appear only as a witness.

I set Baby on the road up to Zurich. There I checked in at the Eden-sur-Lac and then arranged a dinner meeting and council of war at the Café zur Kronenhalle, my favorite Zurich eating place, where I assembled all the Zurich financial giants I knew. It happened that they owed me favors, and Erridge had come to collect.

When I told them what Gaspard had been doing, they were suitably horrified. Their reaction was identical with Hilaire's, except that they felt none of the terror. These were stout fellows. Gaspard Lapointe could be no threat to them. They hastened to tell me that I was doing them the favor, and were unanimous in their decision that Gaspard had to be taught a harsh lesson. One did not play such games with the Swiss banking system. It was a crime against Swiss banking, a crime against the country, and a crime against the stability of world finance. Such crimes must not go unpunished, and they were relishing the prospect of hauling Gaspard Lapointe out to the woodshed.

They then outlined for me a scheme of market manipulations that would be aimed at all of his holdings. In this way they planned to hit the man where he lived. They told me to make Hilaire and nobody else privy to their plans. If these were too widely known, the word would get back to Gaspard and it would only be fresh profits for him. That would never do. That they would be punishing the other Geneva bankers, with the sole exception of Hilaire, along with Gaspard, they considered no more than suitable. The Genevans were to be condemned, for over the years they had been condoning such behavior and fattening themselves with the crumbs that dropped from Gaspard's table.

I gave myself a night in the luxury of the Eden-sur-Lac and then returned to Geneva. When I called on Hilaire and brought him up to date on the success of my overtures in Zurich, he was delighted—and he was terrified. That he was to be greatly enriched by the operations of the Zurichers was most gratifying, but he was troubled by the thought that he would be pulling in something not too far divorced from blood money.

The hearing into the gendarme's guilt was scheduled, and Georges and I were summoned to attend. Things went badly for Arnin. His crimes were too blatant when they stood revealed. He had further compounded them with his greed. Since it is understood among policemen that any take is to be shared among them, the fact that over the years he had been raking it in and sharing nothing was an unforgivable breach of trust. Arnin had not a single colleague who would stand up for him.

My neighbor and I, nevertheless, were placing ourselves in some degree of jeopardy. Cops the world over resent any revelations that besmirch their service; they consider these to be a blot on all of them. Although they will place the heaviest blame on the perpetrator, that does nothing to make them pleased with the informants. They would of course be more on my back than my neighbor's—that I could expect. I was the foreign meddler who stuck his nose into French police affairs; they couldn't take kindly to that. Neither my neighbor nor I, nevertheless, was much worried. Since neither of us had been contemplating the commission of any crimes, we had every reason to expect that we would be all right and that in time the gendarmes' wounds would heal.

Gaspard, surprisingly, appeared as a character witness for the gendarme. He extolled the man to the skies and this should have counted for a great deal: Gaspard pulled a lot of weight in official circles on both sides of the border. Great as it was, however, it was by no means enough. The weight of the evidence was too overwhelming.

At the trial, I had news from my neighbor. He told me that Hilaire had bought the de Montbard house. He was pleased: he expected that Hilaire would be a pleasanter neighbor than Henri-Edouard had been.

CHAPTER 7

The next time I had occasion to listen in on the two killers, it was Erridge who was under discussion. They were toying with the idea of disposing of that nuisance. They needed some way of compensating themselves for the frustrations I had caused them. They were giving no consideration to anything so lurid as castration, but murder was not without its appeal. I could not help but be gratified that they found the prospect of murdering good old Matthew somewhat less alluring than giving Gaspard the treatment.

I followed them again that night but, since their nightly game was only more of the same, I hit the road for the border and went home to bed. During the night I woke to the thought that I had the whole operation ass-backward.

I never have set much store by nighttime inspirations: if they don't stay with you and come back at you with your breakfast croissant, they are not worth remembering. This one, however, did stay with me. It just wasn't possible that Gaspard could have bought the de Montbard diamonds. That much of it Albert must have gotten wrong. Lapointe must have obtained them by some other means.

But then why would he have paid the killers? However inadequate the payment might have been, he had made it; and that was just not in Gaspard's nature. When he put money out, he got full value for it. I had observed this for myself and there was not one of his Geneva colleagues who could not attest to it as well.

It was apparent, then, that his confederates had brought him in on the operation only after the murders of the garbage collector and Henri-Edouard de Montbard. Gaspard could never have been deceived by the gold-in-the-garbage ploy. Great sums of gold or other valuables could not have been moved about without his having had knowledge of it. His intelligence network was notoriously efficient.

I took myself across the line to Geneva and paid him a morning visit. I found him just out of bed, and he had not been alone. His bedfellow was one of the murderers. That he was also sharing his bed with bedbugs and lice was quickly evident. Both of them were scratching.

He was only grudging in his welcome. I had a try at bringing some warmth into it by suggesting that I might have an interest in buying some of the diamonds. I told him that I would have liked to buy all of them, but that I feared he would drive too hard a bargain for me.

"What makes you think you can afford even one of them?" he asked.

"The retainer for the dam should be at least that good," I said.

"There is an excellent possibility, mon ami, that

there will be no retainer. You've been making me unhappy with you."

"I'm truly sorry for that. What would you have had me do?"

"You went to Paris in the hope of finding your garbage. Did you so much as ask for it?"

"No, I didn't. I had lost interest in it."

"That was a mistake. To become so quickly bored indicates a certain flightiness of mind."

"In whose opinion?"

"In mine, for one."

"Before you do anything hasty about the diamonds," I continued, "I would appreciate it if you would keep my interest in mind."

"I fail to understand your interest. Could you explain it?"

"It is sentimental. Although Mme de Montbard was unforgettable, I still would like to have a souvenir, something in the way of a suitable memento."

With that I left. On my way out of the place I made friends with the dogs, amiable beasts, great tail-waggers. There was another guard on the gate: there had evidently been a change. This one was a surly brute, and I made no attempt at setting up friendly relations with him.

I went off to call on Hilaire. He was already up and about, possibly because he had been sleeping alone. I congratulated him on his acquisition of the de Montbard lake house and wished him happiness in the occupancy of it. He was still mourning my loss of the de Montbard dowry, and when I brought up the subject of the diamonds Hilaire was right in there with sympathetic understanding. Here was a man who was not dead to sentiment. But he was discouraging. I could imagine that Gaspard would be asking an extortionate price.

"He did not get them cheaply, and Gaspard has never been known to take less than a usurer's profit."

I was paying this call on Hilaire because I was determined not to give up on my attempt to induce him to move against the formidable Gaspard.

"All right. You don't trust the Zurich crowd," I said, "but what about Wall Street? I am not without friends, Hilaire; I could help you form an alliance there."

"I do not like to speak ill of your friends, Matthew, particularly since they are also your countrymen, but I must tell you that the Wall Streeters are a giddy lot. They are unaccountable."

I thought back to Wall Streeters I knew and "giddy" seemed a strange adjective to lay on them. "Unaccountable" I could accept, but "giddy" was beyond me.

Hilaire insisted on taking me to lunch, and we ran into Gaspard in the restaurant, lunching alone. To my great joy he was still scratching. There were limits to even that great man's immunities. I warned Hilaire against coming within louse-jumping distance, and Hilaire was much amused. He took Gaspard's choice of bedfellow as a hopeful sign. "He might well be murdered," he said.

But Gaspard was looking much too smug. Any possibility of deflating the pompous ass was irresistible, and Erridge is no man to resist the irresistible. I had to make a try at putting a needle into him.

"We have been plotting your downfall, my dear Gaspard," I said.

I should never have done it. Hilaire turned white. He was no David ready to tackle this Goliath and, after all, he had indicated as much to me.

"You and who else?" Gaspard asked.

I hastened to take Hilaire off the hook. "Just me."

"Do you really think you're man enough?"

"Speaking of that—since you are—I don't care for the company you are keeping. And on the subject of company, I'd rather you didn't stand so close. I suggest that you have yourself deloused."

Gaspard laughed. "He said they were healthy."

"Feeding on you, they will be," I said.

He turned back to his own food, scratching all the while. Then he sent a bottle of wine across with the suggestion that we drink to his downfall. I did the drinking. Hilaire had suddenly become a teetotaller; he wouldn't touch the wine. He was genuinely frightened of Gaspard.

"You shouldn't have said that to him," he said. "He is an unforgiving man."

"I took the whole thing on myself, Hilaire, so relax. Gaspard doesn't frighten me."

"You might be well advised to learn some healthy fear, my friend."

"That I would rather not do."

When we parted, Hilaire was happy to see me go. For him the luncheon had been a disaster. I was leaving him disposed to dispense with my company for a while. It was regrettable, but I'd had my fun. I headed back to the Grand Alp. It was time that I caught up with the murderers again. I couldn't leave them too long neglected.

They were in the room next door and they were quarreling. The charge was infidelity, and that was a surprise. But with the thieves falling out, I saw the possibility of divide and conquer. Gaspard seemed a well-fleshed bone of contention but it was not surprising that they might be competing for his favors. It was not possible, however, that they should remain long at odds. The pull of the flesh was too potent. Their quarrel dissolved into other activities and I had eavesdropped on these before. Whatever novelty they might once have held for me had long since been exhausted. I took myself back home, with all chance of dividing and conquering down the drain: the bonds of shared crime were strong, but those of affection were even stronger.

CHAPTER 8

Despite the long planning session, the campaign the Zurich crowd concocted did not greatly appeal to me—it seemed far too devious and complicated, freighted with too many twists and turns, and at any one of them it was likely to go astray. I should have preferred something simpler and more direct; I could go for the hammer blow. The subtlety of their approach worried me. They were quick to assure me, however, that they knew what they were doing. They knew how to ruin a man and Gaspard was to be well punished for his presumption. Nobody could be permitted to play fast and loose with the sacred integrity of the Swiss banking system. They were preparing to dig him a hole out of which he would never be able to climb back up, to the daylight. That they promised me.

With regard to my dam, they laughed at Gaspard's threats. There had never been the means available in Geneva to cover the whole of the financing. Zurich was needed in order to secure adequate funds. Since Zurich could swing it without any assistance from Geneva, the job was mine for the taking. Without Zurich, Gaspard would be nowhere.

Once we had arrived at an agreement, I had another night in the luxury of the Eden-sur-Lac and then headed back home. I did not rate the return as an expulsion from Paradise—my lakeside flat wasn't all that bad.

I made a brief stop, first, to fill Hilaire in on the success of my venture with the Zurich bankers. He was delighted, even though he was still considerably frightened. The prospect of bringing Gaspard down held a strong appeal for him but he didn't quite dare let himself believe in it.

At home I lunched on the terrace. With all my dashing about, I had been neglecting the home cooking, and, since Mme Douvaine was unflagging in her operations at the stove, the freezer was in danger of becoming overstocked.

Refreshed, I returned to the Hôtel du Grand Alp, where I picked up on the killers before they went forth on another of their nights out. They were joined in their room by Arnin, who was quick to warn them against me. I was a dangerous man, and I knew too much. Gaspard had cautioned him against me. They had made a serious mistake in involving me. Stealing my garbage and searching my apartment had been exercises in futility. The only possible advantage in it for them had been the acquisition of my revolver. That, at least, had given the gendarme a handle over me. But even that had come to nothing. They might just as well have spared themselves the bother. For the safety of the lot of them, it might well be time that they set themselves the task of killing Erridge. Unfortunately for them, I was an American, and killing

Americans was something that oughtn't be done lightly.

"They kill each other all the time," the gendarme said, "but what they allow themselves they do not permit to others. You can count on their embassy kicking up the most powerful stink over it."

It wouldn't matter whether they did it one side of the border or the other, although he would be grateful if they managed it on the Swiss side, where it would be out of his jurisdiction. Since it was on official record that he was keeping an eye on me, it would do his career no good if I were to be knocked off right under his nose.

The killers told Arnin that they had been considering doing me in but that it would have to wait until the time was ripe. It must be an operation of the greatest delicacy which would require careful planning and the full cooperation of Gaspard and himself, both of whom had been holding themselves too much aloof from the rough stuff. In the game they were playing, it was wrong that Lapointe and Arnin should be going so long unblooded. One might have thought that they were out in the hunting field discussing the initiation of a tyro.

When the three moved they took themselves down toward the lake. It was a no-nonsense evening, wholly dedicated to profit. And they were no longer permitting the gendarme to play the observer until it was time for the three-way split: it could have been a rehearsal for the Erridge murder, although it was merely rolling drunks and mugging strollers. Around the perimeter of the Palais des Nations they did very well. Tipsy diplomats were abundant and they missed nobody.

When I pulled out and went home to bed, sleep did not come readily.

I breakfasted on the terrace and fed myself too lavishly. That was something I was going to have to watch. It was just no good to substitute gluttony for lechery. I would be letting down both Albert and myself.

Later, I went over to Geneva and paid Gaspard another call. I found him in a foul humor, which might have been because he'd been sleeping alone. He was still scratching, and I thought he might now have been satisfied—but he seemed to require more.

"Was your Zurich trip a success?" he inquired.

It could have been no more than a polite inquiry, but I was not so dull as to take it for simply that. He was putting me on notice that his intelligence network was still in operation and that I could never make even the first move which would not be under his scrutiny. It seemed astonishing that I should have been able to go on for so long without his having become aware of my taking the room at the Grand Alp. In that area he appeared to have had something of an intelligence breakdown.

Now he put on an air of great solicitude. Doing me out of the dam job had been the outside limit of

THE GARBAGE COLLECTOR 109

the punishment he had chosen for me: a total
wrecking of my career had not been in his reckon-
ing. I allowed myself the fun of indicating to him
that I was still very much in the running for the
dam project. He pretended to be not much impressed. "I was given to understand that Zurich
will not need Geneva," I said. "They can swing it
entirely on their own. So you are not about to be
needed—or feared."

"In other words, you think you sucked up to
them successfully?"

"I don't suck, Gaspard. That's your department.
I can tell you that Zurich is not pleased with you."

"Screw Zurich," Gaspard said.

"If you are so stupid that you think you *can*," I
retorted.

That afternoon the wheels began to turn. The
effects showed up in the quotations on the Geneva
Bourse. Everything that Gaspard held was selling
off and he was soon scrambling for cover. He came
across the border to seek me out. He was now
ready to make a deal on the de Montbard diamonds. The man was so desperate that he was even
ready to consider a sale to me, and he was offering
them at an astonishingly moderate price.

I wasn't having any.

I told him that I had gotten the better of my
sentimental feelings. I was again the hardheaded
American engineer, and he was going to have to
peddle his loot elsewhere. He sweetened his offer,

but he just couldn't interest me. I had made up my mind: I was not in the market for diamonds, not his or any others. The man was crawling, and it was a most pleasing spectacle. I thoroughly enjoyed it.

As soon as I was shut of Gaspard, I went into a huddle with Georges Bardelot. The time had come again to enlist his cooperation, and I found him more than willing. He was even eager. The next step in the campaign, I had decided, was to be the breakup of the evil cabal. Strategy called for hitting them where they were the most vulnerable, and that would be by mounting an attack on gendarme Arnin. He was wide open on a variety of charges not yet pressed but which I had meanwhile discovered. On conspiracy I wanted to hold off for a while. It was too soon to be tipping my hand. You can't attack one party to a conspiracy and leave the other participants untouched. Gaspard had to wait on the good offices of the Zurich bankers.

My revelations of the gendarme's misdeeds evoked from Georges a quite suitable degree of horror. Again he was to bring the charges; I was serving only as a witness to the crimes.

Keeping the peace in this border area depended on a close cooperation between the Swiss and French gendarmeries. Constabulary duties were shared and I gathered that, if there should be anything in the way of graft, that would likewise be shared. Arnin's having held much of the take for himself—once again—constituted therefore a "breach of contract" not to be forgiven. That the victims had, in large number, been diplomatic personnel added greatly to gravity of his and the other gendarmes' crimes. Strong representations, I had learned, had been made to the Swiss Foreign Office, and the frowns of the Soviet, British, French, and American embassies could not be taken lightly. It pleased the Swiss Foreign Office mightily that in their response to the diplomatic representations they could say, now, that the malefactor had not been Swiss but French and that the French Ministry of Justice was performing in exemplary fashion. The men, including Arnin, were to be well punished.

It went without saying, of course, that my neighbor and I would do well to step lightly thereafter. We could have, now, even less expectation of being popular with the gendarmes—on either side of the border.

Returning to Geneva following this second case against the gendarme, I explored the effect my move had had on the two killer-conspirators. They were tougher than I had realized: they took it with great good humor. Apart from some concern over the intimate knowledge I'd been able to show of their every move, they were rather gleeful over Arnin's downfall. That there had been no pity in them I could have expected, but I'd been anticipating some sort of healthy concern for their own hides. Instead, they were taking only a financial view of this turn in events. They had not been happy with the three-way split. It would now be half and half, and that suited them far better.

I called on Gaspard. He was most welcoming, but only because he thought I'd been having second thoughts and had come to negotiate for the diamonds, which were still unsold. When I told him that I'd had no resurgence of sentiment, he turned surly.

He, too, had had the news of the gendarme. The man, not unexpectedly, had once more appealed to Gaspard's protective power. When that power proved insufficient to cover crimes of such appalling dimensions, all Arnin had had from Gaspard was an unwelcome lecture on overreaching himself. If he had responded by threatening Gaspard with exposure, the threat had worried Gaspard not at all. Any exposure of Gaspard could not be accomplished without equal exposure of his own not inconsiderable role in the de Montbard affair, and Gaspard knew that the gendarme, no matter how desperate, was not yet ready to cut his own throat. Conspirators have always been notoriously unreliable witnesses.

My next targets would need to be the two murderers. Meanwhile, Gaspard would have to be left standing alone. In tackling Gaspard I knew what I was undertaking, and later, with Zurich to back me up, I had every confidence that I could bring it off.

I went to Hilaire and told him of my recent accomplishment. I had to boast to someone about my exploit. But it served only to give the poor guy the shakes. He refused to believe that I was not playing with fire. And for some never-to-be-explained reason, he had now come to thoroughly distrust Zurich. Those bankers up there were going to stab Erridge in the back and Hilaire didn't want to see that. He had no cause for believing anything else.

Hilaire, as a matter of fact, should have been overjoyed. He had profited tidily from the fall in Gaspard's stocks. In any case, he insisted that my operations up in Zurich had triggered the fall and that I had alerted him to expect it, and he was all for splitting his profits with me. The idiot was seeing it as blood money and was bent on lightening his guilt by unloading at least some of it on Erridge.

A sizable fortune was mine for the taking, and it could easily have covered the price of some of the de Montbard diamonds. Those Swiss bankers don't play with pennies. But though I didn't want it, Hilaire, it turned out, had already deposited it in my account. He regretted that it was less than what I would have had from the de Montbard dowry; but, over my every protest, he insisted that there would be more to come. If I was so stupid that I didn't want it, I could donate it to my favorite charity.

"I understand Americans are in the habit of doing that. It is a strange habit, but then nobody ever said that Americans were not strange."

Stupidly, I could not rid *myself* of the feeling that it was blood money. I could tell myself that I had been doing no more than oiling the wheels of justice, but I was only too well aware of the delights of revenge. I could hardly go on reveling in it without developing some degree of awareness.

I could think of nothing that might have been suitably done with the money, unless it were to erect a memorial to Mathilde de Montbard. It would need to be something like a scholarship for the study of the *Ars Amatoria;* she had, after all, been a most avid disciple of Ovid.

Hilaire, at this juncture, was busily preparing for a blockbuster of a housewarming. It was to be a whing-ding that would make the old de Montbard parties seem like nothing more than prayer meetings. He was debating whether or not he should be retaining Gaspard on the guest list. The problem arose from the fact that Gaspard had always been the *arbiter elegantiae* in these parts: he had always set the requirements of protocol. But when a man was on the skids, there was an exquisitely determined point at which he was deemed to have gone far enough in his descent from glory to be stricken from party lists. However, for Hilaire to act too soon would establish him as being unfeeling; if he acted too late, he would be condemned for being unperceptive. The moment had to be judged to a nicety. Committing an error either way would be taken as an indication of a lack of acumen: it would be interpreted as meaning that Hilaire was insufficiently privy to the thinking up in Zurich. Since Hilaire lacked confidence in Zurich, his situation was grave.

I left him to his problems. Apart from trying to bolster his faith in the determination of the Zurich bankers, I could do little for him. He had to sweat it out on his own.

I was concerned with exactly how I was to engineer my next move. In the interest of good fun, I might have liked to arrange matters so that the murderous pair could be apprehended in Gaspard's bed, but that had obvious drawbacks. It would require that I accuse them of their old crimes, and I was going to have to leave it to the gendarmes to build the charges up to encompass the three murders, which I expected would come with the arrest of Gaspard. He wouldn't be taking the rap for that part of the deal.

For starters I was planning to make do with the pair's muggings and the rollings, but I would be asked why I had delayed putting in my report on them, and that was a question I was not prepared to answer. I would do better to wait till the two again went out on the town and blow the whistle on them in time to have them caught red-handed.

The arrest of Arnin having belatedly opened their eyes to the hazards of working on diplomatic personnel, they concluded that they had been operating in Geneva too long, and switched their base of operations to Annemasse. I couldn't have been more pleased. Annemasse is the one sizable town on the French side in that border area. Having them give France a workout was perfect for my purposes. Since they would be apprehended in France, a great deal of awkwardness would be eliminated. When the time came for the charges against them to be upped to include the three murders, they would be neatly in the right jurisdiction.

They began the night's activities by stealing a car. For a moment this looked as though it might prove unfortunate for me, but I managed to flag down a cab and I had him follow. I was prepared to do the whole run by cab. Of course, I didn't know then that it was to be all the way to Annemasse, but that would have made no difference. Conveniently enough, our route out of the city went past the place where I had parked Baby. As luck would have it—and don't tell me that luck wasn't with me that night—I happened to have found a parking place on the street, something that is not often possible in Geneva. I could, therefore, make the switch from cab to Baby in nothing flat.

If I did lose a tick in making the swap, the Porsche was quick to pick it up. Soon I found myself pitying the owner of the stolen car: they drove with more dash than skill, and he was likely to get his bus back with the smoothest set of gears in automotive history.

In Annemasse they parked and went prowling on foot. I prowled with them. It wasn't long before they spotted their quarry, though even on first sight it seemed to me they were making a bad mistake: the lad was too big by half, and too burly. They might have done better with a chap who had less of that look of being able to take care of himself. They did, it's true, have the advantage of numbers but they should have known that numbers are not all.

They moved in on the guy in the classic manner: one of them came up behind him and flung his arm around his throat; the other came at him from the front and buried his fist in the guy's belly. As I'd expected, it was a hard belly. The first just bounced off it and the lad didn't crumple. His own fist zeroed in on his assailant's belly and found there an area that was a great deal softer. The bastard crumpled. He was at least temporarily out of the action.

The guy who had taken our laddie from the rear, however, was more of a problem. The lad tried to shake loose but had no success. For the moment they had reached an impasse. They flailed around. There was no spare hand now for diving into the boy's pockets. That needed the recovery of the second man—and he was coming back quickly.

This seemed the suitable moment for Erridge to step in and do his stuff. I whistled loud and, coming in behind the man who was keeping his stranglehold on the lad, I indulged myself. I did something I had been wanting to do for a long time: I kicked him in the ass. If he had been a freestanding target I would have punted him all the way back into Switzerland. It was a soul-satisfying moment.

The goon released the lad and whirled around to confront this fresh challenge. He could not have done me a greater favor. I began by bloodying his nose and followed by blacking one eye. Luckily, where we were it was too dark for him to see what had caught up with him, but it did seem a pity that he shouldn't know it was Erridge getting his own back. With that in mind I left him the other eye intact. A healthy clip to the chin then put him away.

I turned to see how the lad was getting along with his man. He was giving an excellent account of himself. He needed no helping hand from Erridge or anyone else. He was handy with his fists and he was making every punch count. It was going to be a good long time before either of those babies would be pretty to look at.

Gendarmes showed up in response to my whistle and we turned the two over to them. The lot of us moved to the gendarmerie, where we preferred the necessary charges. I suggested that the Swiss gendarmes would have an interest. I was saying nothing about the murders. The time for that would come later. The gendarmes congratulated us on our performance and praised us for our valor and courage, not to speak of our prowess.

It turned out that my young friend was something of a celebrity—in fact, a local hero. He was a footballer and that gave us something in common, even though mine was the American game and his was soccer. I asked him to have dinner with me and after a considerable argument over who would stand whom, I finally won him over. He suggested an Annemasse restaurant which, he said, was locally thought well of, but I had Le Père Bise in mind and that did it. I couldn't consider being this close to Talloires and eating anywhere else. He had never been there, but of course he had heard of it.

We ate well and drank well and talked about the World's Cup. When I happened to mention that my home, when I was there, was in New Jersey, the kid just flipped. Had I ever seen the great Pelé play? I had. So I was touched with stardust. We topped the food off with a cognac older than our combined ages, and I drove him home to An-nemasse.

At his house the American footballer had to be introduced to the kid's dad, with a fully dramatized reenactment of the way our hero had rescued him from the two vicious muggers. The old man would not let me go until I first shared a bottle of wine with them. It was a good wine. For his son's Amer-ican champion it had to be nothing but the best.

By the time I could break away and turn Baby's nose back toward the lake, they had me pleasantly buzzed. Not to put too fine a point on it, Erridge was zonked. Baby and I were a menace to safety on the roads that night, but the providence that watches over fools and drunkards was with us all the way and we made it without damage. I reeled up the stairs to the flat and fell into bed, feeling full of booze and good works.

In the morning I had a visit from the gendarmes. Making a formal ceremony of the occasion, the gendarmes were returning my revolver to me. They had recovered it from the killers' Grand Alp retreat along with various and sundry other loot. As I expected, it was serving to put them back on the track of the three murders. If it hadn't been the revolver, of course, it would have been something else. But it was quite satisfactory to me that it should be my revolver. Up to this point I'd been thinking that it was hardly worth all the trouble I had been to for bringing it into the country with me.

The gendarmes had yet to make the Gaspard connection, for the bully boys had not yet begun to talk. They were still counting on Gaspard's power to come to their rescue.

Shortly after the gendarmes left me, my neighbor, Bardelot, came to call. He had always had an insatiable curiosity about any gendarme activity, but now, when there was some possibility it might involve him, his curiosity was on a more practical footing. Georges was relieved to learn that they had come only to return my revolver, and it seemed to me that he was doubly relieved, since he'd been uncomfortable at the thought of my going along without a gun. It had been his opinion that Erridge was living dangerously.

Georges was fully informed of my activities of the night before (not, perhaps, of my drunkenness, although it might have been tact that kept him from mentioning that). The attempted mugging of the footballer had been headline news for the local paper and the provincial TV. To have made such an attempt on an Annemasse hero was rated as being a gross example of lèse majesté. It was considered consummately suitable that the man who had come to the lad's aid should have been a renowned American footballer. The "renowned" crept in there in an interview with the young chappie's father, who had conferred on me a degree of fame I'd never earned.

The combat was depicted as having been far bloodier and much more hazardous than it was, and my neighbor was not the man to make allowances for journalistic exaggeration. I tried to set him right, but he would listen to no amendments. Georges liked the myth just as it was; he didn't want it disturbed. To his way of thinking, it would confer a degree of distinction on himself. Embarrassing as this was, I was forced to leave it that way, particularly since I knew I was destined to be a source of disappointment to the good man before we would be writing finish to this affair.

Now that I again had my revolver in hand, he was expecting me to make good use of it. After all, what good was there in having an American neighbor if one were not to have the pleasure of witnessing a good, old-fashioned, American-style, Chicago, cinematic shoot-'em-up? Whom I was to shoot was for Georges a minor consideration.

The Geneva Bourse was, meanwhile, in a state of wild confusion. Rescue had come to Gaspard from an unpredictable source: the American banks had stepped in to buy, boosting Gaspard's securities to a succession of new highs. I'd been forewarned of this possibility by my Zurich allies and had passed the warning on to Hilaire Talbot. The American bankers, as he had feared, were proving to be a "giddy" lot; but Hilaire was not holding that against me. Having switched his positions just in time, he was coming out with another monumental profit. His pockets were fattening as satisfactorily as were Gaspard's.

This reprieve, of course, was no more than temporary. Zurich was holding fast. They claimed to be as reliable as the Rock of Gibraltar, and they were every bit of that. They were bouncing the quotations up and down and, with the warnings of the fluctuations that I was in a position to pass on to him, Hilaire was profiting with every bounce. That he was inflexible in his insistence on my profiting along with him was something I couldn't control. My monument to the memory of Mathilde de Montbard was well on its way toward growing into a blockbuster.

This turn in Gaspard's fortunes, even though it was to be only temporary, served to lift Hilaire out of his dilemma: Gaspard was not to be dropped from the guest list. It would be unfortunate if he were to bring his infestation of lice with him, but it was to be hoped that sometime before the party he would have submitted himself to a delousing. I was not sorry that he was to be there. He had a good, fat ass to bring to the wind surfing, and that was a spectacle I had every expectation of enjoying.

I went over to Geneva and paid Gaspard a visit. Even though he had evidently been sleeping alone, he was riding high. For a man who was an old hand at the ebb and flow of market manipulation, he had turned fantastically and, I thought, unaccountably naïve. It did not seem possible that he wasn't aware of the fact that the game was up. He had been stripped of his allies. He had lost control of the market. Although Zurich had not quite shown its hand, there had certainly been indications and he should have been picking up on them. His failure of awareness could not be attributed to stupidity or inexperience. It had to be born of arrogance. If he had not previously known there were limits to his might and power, the fall of the gendarme and of the pair of murderers should have been a more than adequate demonstration of his vulnerability, but such, of course, is the nature of hubris. (Without it there could have been no Greek tragedy.)

It was with the greatest gratification that I was at long last in a position, on this visit to Geneva, to give up my room at the Grand Alp.

I needed, now, to do another jaunt up to Zurich to satisfy myself of the intentions of the banking community there. I had to know what, to their way of thinking, might be the first order of business. Was it to be playing cute games on the Bourse to my profit and Hilaire's and causing a yo-yoing up and down in Gaspard's financial standing—or had they reached the stage where they would be prepared to get serious about bringing on the destruction of Lapointe?

It may be that I had, to some extent, become infected with Hilaire's doubts about their steadfastness. I was not feeling any of his terror of Gaspard's power, but distrust of bankers is a built-in part of every engineer's consciousness. They should give courses in it at engineering school, but all of us get it as part of our on-the-job training. I have lived and worked too much with Europeans and Asians to have any standard American distrust of all foreigners, but my feeling about bankers knows nothing of national boundaries. I package the Americans in with the rest. The slickness of many American businessmen may reasonably be considered an American export. They are all a lot of smoothies, too smooth by half.

I set up another council of war at the Kronenhalle. They were all there and they came on strong with their reassurances. It was only a matter of timing, they said, and I was going to have to leave to them. They were doing it by the clock—and doesn't the whole world know how good the Swiss are in the clock department? Clocks may not be cheese or chocolate but they come mighty close.

They were happy to hear that I'd been pulling a profit out of their manipulations, and they were all for my continuing to take Hilaire into my confidence. Good old Hilaire Talbot was a solid man.

He was to be trusted. They were quick, however, to caution me against letting my trust run away with me. The other Geneva bankers might appear to be stout fellows, but they had been too thoroughly trained in dancing to Gaspard's tune. They were not unaware that they were undertaking a course that was calculated to lead to the downfall of the complete Geneva banking structure and that they could be in the process of building an international calamity. They asked me to believe them when they insisted that they would not permit that to happen. Swiss international credit was far too important to them: they were not planting land mines under their own financial foundations. I was to trust their acumen that far. At the proper time they would be passing the word, and the boys down in Geneva would be bailing out.

What they were to do about the American bankers they were leaving up to me. They had not taken kindly to the imbecile Americans who had intruded to reverse the trend Zurich had set up and had done so at a time that had inconvenienced Zurich. They were of a mind to punish the Americans, to hit them right in their business school know-how. One thing stood in the way: they would be obliged to bring down along with the Americans the British, the French, the Germans, the Italians, and just about everyone else.

"We can't get the word out to those others and not have a leak go to the Americans," one Zuricher said. "And we can't very well smash the whole of international finance. You don't destroy your customers—that's never been good business."

This was heady stuff, putting it into my hands to determine the fate of banking the world over. I couldn't tell them simply to go ahead and smash up the whole damn thing and they knew it. I had to say go easy on the Americans.

It was intoxicating. They had me sitting with them in the seats of power. I wondered whether the sweet old parties who were layering the herring filets on the blocks of ice and setting out the bowls of *crème fraîche* could possibly know that, even as I fed at their board, I was holding in my two hands the financial future of the civilized world. Then I set that speculation aside for one more immediate. I asked myself if all the cream would necessarily be in the bowls—if Erridge were not being smeared with some of it, too. There was, after all, more than a touch of the good old carrot-and-stick in the line they'd been feeding me.

I was then told myself that the Zurich bankers had no way of knowing anything of my resentment of the business school laddies. That was something I had been keeping to myself; and, in any event, it would have been beyond their understanding. They could never have guessed that they had been holding temptation up before me. It was far more likely they were under the impression that they had been threatening me.

In parting the Zurichers loaded me down with messages for Hilaire. But they had me in above my head in no time flat, throwing at me intricacies and elaborations that were totally beyond me. I am not a mathematical imbecile: differential calculus, in my engineer's mind, jumps through hoops. And the fancy footwork they had engaged in earlier had never been beyond me; I'd relayed it to Hilaire with never a hitch. Now, however, these babies had Erridge roped and tied. I had them repeat, and I had to take notes. Without some measure of comprehension, memory simply lies down and dies.

While they assured me, finally, that they knew exactly how they were going to make this financial fandango work, they were leaving me with a flock of nagging doubts. I could see no way that it wouldn't be tripping over its own feet and falling flat on its overelaborated face. For one thing, it seemed to me what Gaspard must surely recognize that prices couldn't put themselves through anything so outrageously fancy unless somebody was up there to pull the strings. It seemed to me that it was one of those things that might take so many twists and turns that it would be meeting itself coming back.

CHAPTER 9

So, then, it was back again to the lake for an interval of watchful waiting.

On the way, I made a quick stop at the Bourse to pass on to Hilaire the complex instructions I brought down from Zurich. He grabbed them with unmitigated joy. These were just the sort of convoluted manipulations that were Hilaire's idea of fun and games. I also passed on to him the warning I'd had from our Zurich allies: he was not to take any of his Geneva confrères into his confidence. "They trust you and they say that they believe in me," I said. "But none of the rest of the boys! They want to be certain that you will be playing it close to the chest."

Hilaire had some misgivings on that account. He was not of a mind to be a willing party to the destruction of the Geneva Bourse. "It will be like putting a bomb under the place. They can't ask me to do that."

I was able to assure him that Zurich was not unaware of the dangers inherent in the game they were playing. "When the time comes, they will be passing the word. The Swiss banking structure will be left standing fast. Even the Americans, however undeserving they may be, will come out of it undamaged."

Despite his mistrust of the Zurich crowd, Hilaire

took me at my word. I had to hope that I would not be leading him astray. I was the one who had faith in Zurich. Meanwhile, he had news for me. As a result of the market coup he'd pulled off during the American intervention, Gaspard was again in the chips.

Once he was back in funds, Lapointe had upped his price on the de Montbard diamonds to his earlier exorbitant level. Since the cut-price offer had been made to nobody but Erridge, and I had kept it to myself, he had been making a series of sales and enriching himself mightily. The ladies of Geneva would be going about in splendor, and it could be expected that the glitter would be blinding. According to Hilaire, this was perhaps beyond my imagining, since I had never seen Mathilde de Montbard in her glory.

"Gaspard is going to celebrate," Hilaire told me. "He is putting on one of his galas. White tie, tailcoats, Dom Pérignon, caviar and foie gras. He asked me to tell you that you are on his guest list."

I didn't know quite what to make of that, except that it was not to my liking. I can guzzle the vintage champagne and slurp up the caviar and foie gras with the best of them, but I had my Zurich buddies to think about. I didn't care to have them come down with any notion that Erridge might be wavering. They could scarcely suspect me of being locked into Gaspard's orbit, but I knew that bunch and I was well aware of the low esteem in which they held Americans. They give us credit for little brain, and they could easily come to believe that Gaspard was taking me into camp. Yet for me to decline the invitation would be to show my hand prematurely, and Gaspard would not be slow to read the signs. To disdain attendance in Gaspard's ballroom would be too clear a declaration. I had no choice but to go. I might even make a try at enjoying myself.

At home I found another invitation awaiting me. Apparently Erridge was going to have a busy social season. This one came from the father of the footballer, asking me to join him in Annemasse to watch his son out on the field. It would be no more than a provincial game, with Annemasse pitted against Annecy—and of that the old man was regretful. He promised, however, that in its small way it would be good sport and that his son could be expected to acquit himself well. This invitation, I can tell you, held far greater appeal for me than the elegantly engraved job that craved my attendance at Gaspard's gala. The footballer's dad was good company. I liked his spirit, his gusto, and his wine. Watching football has always been in my book the next best thing to playing it. Annemasse vs. Annecy would be played for blood, and I was quite in the mood for blood.

The two events were scheduled for different evenings, so there would be no conflict there, although I might have preferred it if there had been. My football game could have served as an excellent excuse for dodging Gaspard's gala.

The game was set for that same night, so I phoned my acceptance. My buddy, the postmaster, was greatly interested. He was also going to the game. He was an ardent Annemasse rooter. I hadn't known anyone half so rahrah since my prep school days. He promised me great excitement. My young friend was the star of the Annemasse team; I was to expect phenomenal things of the lad.

I tried to persuade papa to permit me to lay on an after-game celebration at Le Père Bise. This, however, was not to be, although he left the door open for doing it at some other date. The traditional after-game celebration was a cut-and-dried affair and attendance at it was mandatory for the players.

All of them who were not in hospital gathered at the Annemasse restaurant his son had recommended on the night of our first meeting. The game would be replayed over food and wine, and absence on the part of the team's star would be bad form. It would be thought that he was snubbing his less talented fellows.

The visiting American footballer was to be an honored guest, said papa. Was he not, after all, a man who had seen the great Pelé play? That fact alone could have been his ticket of admission. That he had come to their hero's assistance made his presence that much more desirable. That he was in his own right a footballer—even if in the corrupted

American variation on the sport—made his attendance no less than mandatory.

It was probably just as well, I thought. It would,
in all likelihood, not have been the right night for
Le Père Bise, who could not have taken kindly to
my bringing the archenemy to dine at his table. He
would, of course, not have poisoned us—that
would not be Le Père Bise's style—but I would
never again have been received in his restaurant
with the kind of welcome that had been mine previously. A later date, when the wounds would have
healed, would be much more sensible.

I climbed into Baby and took myself to Annemasse. Erridge had a ball. The kids played well
and our boy covered himself with glory. I sat with
papa in the stands. And he could not be persuaded
that I could understand any of what was going on.
It was certain to him that American football must
have corrupted me to so great an extent that every
play called for detailed explication, so he provided
a running commentary. That old boy should have
been on TV. He never ran out of words—they
spilled out of him like wine from an overflowing
vat.

If he gave extra wordage and emphasis to the
exploits of his son, that was understandable since
the lad was all over the field and making it look
easy. The old man in his day had been a star in his
own right, and the kid was what he was by right of
inheritance. I'll say this for the old boy: he refrained from laboring his own former stardom. But

it could readily be deduced from the awe and respect shown him by the other rooters. He had not been forgotten.

The after-game party was riotous. The beating our boy had not taken on the field his teammates laid on him in the restaurant. It seemed they would never tire of whacking away at the seat of his pants. The lad would be taking away with him a thoroughly tenderized behind.

As soon as I had been identified as the man who had succored our hero his teammates went into competition in a show of their approbation. They had the honest working man's big, hard, heavy hands powered by magnificently muscled arms. Their handshakes with me illustrated amply. When they whammed a man's bottom, I knew, it must have felt as though they were slugging him with an oak board.

So it was all good clean fun and we demonstrated our toughness by never so much as wincing. There was food enough to provision an army: lake trout and perch, chicken and veal and rabbit, cabbage and turnips and endive, tartes and cakes and ice creams. And there was wine—and they were all sweating it out as fast as they soaked it up.

Cognac came with the coffee, and we drank toasts to everybody and everything. We drank to Annemasse. We drank to our hero and, individually, to his goals. We drank to his father and to the memory of the old boy's footballing exploits. We drank to the humiliation of Annecy and to American football. I had myself a breather while they were drinking to me, which called for a succession of toasts: they drank to the assist I had given the lad; they drank to whatever they may have thought I'd done in my own football days; they drank to the times I had seen Pelé play. I had to tell them precisely how many times it had been, since it was important to them that we drink to each of the times separately.

Despite the great quantities of food I had taken aboard—certainly enough to have soaked up a good part of all that alcohol—Erridge was sozzled. And Erridge is a lad who doesn't sozzle easily. I wasn't under-the-table anesthetized, but I wasn't too far from it. My legs seemed to be of differing lengths and my knees had developed wills of their own. I was wobbling and I was reeling. It was evident that Baby would be best left in her berth till morning, when I would have nothing more than a head to contend with—I've had those all the way out to there, and they are manageable. I was all for finding myself a hotel room for the night.

But my two friends would have none of that. They were matching me, wobble for wobble and reel for reel; but drink, if anything, was making them stubborn. They were taking me home with them. Their house was my house. We could even have another drink when we got there. (The boy evidently trained on the juice.) There was nothing I could do with good grace but yield, and it was not the promise of a nightcap that won me over.

I shared the lad's room, which had an extra bed; Guy had a brother who was off doing his military service. Happily, he didn't snore, although I have a hunch that I was too squiffed to have known if he did. We slept like babies and nobody woke up crying during the night.

Come morning, I was feeling my age.

I lay for a while mourning those happy days when I hadn't known the meaning of the word "hangover." Guy woke and he was happy as a lark. Whistling merrily, he went off to shave. I went looking for dad, craving the company of a fellow sufferer. I can't say he was worse than I was but he wasn't in the mood for whistling either.

He came down on chappie hard for whistling, telling him that he wasn't too big for a whipping, certainly not on a morning when daddy had the American footballer to help him with it. The American footballer was indeed more than ready to lead the way to the woodshed, but now the kid became properly contrite. I can't say that we were frightening him any, but Guy was a good lad, not insensible to human suffering. He made coffee and brought in fresh croissants to us.

Guy was all for frying me six or seven eggs, convinced that no American could survive till noon without eggs. And for an American footballer he thought it would need to be a great many eggs. When I told him that before lunchtime I found eggs intolerable—and that this morning of all mornings I didn't even want to hear of them—he was disappointed in me. I was being un-American.

Before breakfast was over, the three of us indulged ourselves with hair of the dog: we said goodbye and made our date for Le Père Bise and I walked off to pull Baby out of her parking space.

I made the run back to the lake. When I was rolling past the post office, the postmaster came out to accost me. He had to know how much I'd enjoyed the game and he wanted my opinion of it. He was doing research, seeing the game from the point of view of an American footballer. I parked Baby and joined him in the post office. While mail distribution waited, we covered the whole game, play by play.

Back at the house I had it all to do over again with Georges, who was out on the granary's doorstep waiting for his mail. What with the delay Erridge had occasioned, delivery was late that morning, and my neighbor was impatient. He hadn't made it to the game and he was regretting it. A fervent Annemasse rooter, he had to be told all about it, play by play. Somewhat to his astonishment, I was able to oblige.

Hilaire had been out to look over his newly acquired property, and had been invited to his housewarming. The good man was bowled over by this act of graciousness on Hilaire's part. He had expected that Hilaire would be a better neighbor than Henri-Edouard de Montbard but had not been prepared for anything this good. He went on and on about it. Somehow he had come up with the mistaken notion that Erridge had secured the invitation for him. His wife had already gone off to Geneva to buy herself a suitable frock for the festivities. I suggested that a bathing suit might be more to the point, but he was quick to tell me that she was shopping for that as well. He was concerned about his own habiliments since he owned no tailcoat.

"For wind surfing? A tailcoat would only be an impediment."

"Surely it will be something more than wind surfing?" he said.

I was disappointing Georges of his glamorous expectations. I hastened to assure him that there would be more, but that sports attire would be fully adequate, and that seemed to set his fears at rest.

That evening I went into Geneva for Gaspard's gala.

The binge was everything that Hilaire had indicated it would be. The ladies were there and, as he'd promised, they were lavishly bedecked with the diamonds. The displays were dazzling, but not as much as I'd been led to believe. The difference between paste replicas and the real thing is more financial than visible, and the chief difference lay in the fact that I had never seen Mathilde when she was wearing the whole lot. Lack of body space had more likely been the reason for her abstinence, however, than any considerations of taste. Of course a good part of what I was now seeing had been Henri-Edouard's purchases for transfer to Switzerland, and they had never belonged to Mathilde. I should have realized that.

Any concern I might have had over the possibility that Zurich assumed my presence was an indication that I was waffling died a quick death very soon after my arrival. If *they* were concerned about *my* steadfastness, I might with equal validity have been concerned about theirs. They were there in full force. Gaspard was scoring a triumph and he knew it. He was taking all too conspicuous pleasure in parading before me the Zurichers' ostensibly amiable intimacy. A great deal of kissing on both cheeks went on, and much back slapping. Since these were not athletes, there was no rump whacking, but what there was registered as no less a demonstration of approbation.

In the course of the evening's festivities I huddled, nevertheless, with the Zurich bankers. They were not so crude that they would conspire against their host even while they were sucking up his Dom Pérignon, but they kissed me on both cheeks and slapped me on the back. And they did not leave me wanting for guarantees of our solidarity. All the time, as might have been expected, Hilaire was watching. I could suppose that from where he stood it might well have looked as if we were trimming, Zurich and Erridge together.

I did what I could to assuage Hilaire's anxiety. I brought him into the huddle. I kissed his two cheeks. I slapped him on the back. Rarely has my face been so much brushed by whiskers.

Hilaire thanked me for the return of his billfold. It had come back to him empty of the cash, of course, but the papers he had been carrying in it had not been touched and he was delighted to have those back. The billfold had been taken from the pocket of his cloak during Gaspard's previous party, one from which I had been excluded, and it was among the items of loot the gendarmes had taken from the two goons along with my revolver after their arrest in Annemasse. Gratitude for the recovery had to go to Erridge since it was Erridge who had brought about the arrest.

Gaspard, of course, was aware of crimes that might be committed against his guests. Tonight the guard was at his station at the gate complete with shotgun and all guests were required to show their invitations before they were permitted through. Another of the servants was parking the cars, and throughout the evening the barking of the guard dogs was a nonstop accompaniment to the chamber music valiantly contributed by a string quartet in Gaspard's music room. In the ballroom the bedlam the rock band provided for dancing competed more successfully.

I danced with Mme Talbot and with all of the Zurich wives, fulfilling my social obligations in style. Since I was an American, it was expected that I should be up on all the latest sexual gymnastics, and scandals, across the Atlantic. I was forced to explain again and again that I don't get home all that much and that, while I am there, I'm likely to be consorting with the wrong generation for any such shenanigans. I was a major disappointment to the ladies.

Gaspard complimented me on my dancing. For what it was, it wasn't too bad, but it merited no compliments. He was being very attentive, really piling it on. I could not understand what he might be up to, unless he was trying to make his peace— although it might have been that he was entertaining the vain delusion that he could get me to bed.

Later, I said my goodnights and pulled out. As I was leaving, I paused for a few words with the dogs. For all their apparent ferocity, they were amiable beasts and they liked me. I also made a good try with the guard at the gate, offering him a genial goodnight and a generous tip. He pocketed the tip and snarled what might have been "Merci." It could just as easily have been "Merde"; the brute, I'd sensed, didn't care for me, and there was no *pourboire* so large that it would be likely to win him over. I laughed his hostility off; it was certainly of no consequence.

The servant who was handling the parking brought Baby around to the gate. He was a far more friendly type. He had much enjoyed the few yards he'd had the chance of driving her, and he admired her inordinately. The laddie was a con-

noisseur of motor cars and knew a lady when he
had the handling of one.

I was too charged up for any thought of bed. It
was a night when I sincerely mourned Mathilde. I
was a boy badly in need of a girl. It need not have
been one of Mathilde's skills—even one who required instructions would have done nicely. But I
knew none nearer than Paris, and Paris was too
long a jump.

I drove home, but only for long enough to pick
up my skis. Then I returned to Baby and had her
run me up to Chamonix and beyond. There I skied
some of the lower slopes of Mont Blanc and
watched her gleam white in the moonlight. It was
like cooling myself down with an ice cream cone,
but when a man must make do, he does. I wore
myself out skiing and then drove home to bed. The
remedy worked. I slept—not like an innocent babe,
since innocence had been long gone, but like a
rock. And that was good enough.

It was a couple of days later that Hilaire had his
big do. It was a resounding success. He had been
determined to erase all memories of the de
Montbard weekends and he succeeded admirably.
Along the way he also made it a party that eclipsed
Gaspard's gala—and that took a lot of doing.

We water-skied as long as the sun held up, and,
astonishingly, we held up along with the sun.
Hilaire was the ring-tailed expert, and downstairs
my neighbor, Georges, was in every respect his

equal. There were no belly whoppers. Hilaire proved himself to have every right for heaping scorn on Henri-Edouard and his cronies. I couldn't pretend to be competing in their league, but at my own level I did not do too badly. Only once or twice did I smooth the lake surface with my behind.

I had been a witness to the preparations. *Enormous* shipments of food and drink had come out from the Geneva gourmet shops all through the day. The servants had cooked up a storm, and Hilaire's wife had taken a hand in the baking to turn out some of her specialties, so that the entire village was redolent with chocolate.

Mme Douvaine had been lost to me for the day. She was over there, keeping a sharp eye on every move Mme Talbot was making. If up to that time Erridge had been eating well, he could now anticipate a future that would be wall-to-wall chocolate cake. Calories were a language Mme Douvaine neither spoke nor understood and I blessed her for it. The lean days would be coming when I would be out at work on the dam, subsisting on the cooking provided by a camp cook who lived by the fry pan.

There was dancing on the boat dock and far too many dancers for the space available. My neighbor's wife arrived in the gown she'd had made for the occasion, but along with all the others she changed into a bikini and stayed in it throughout the party. This was just as well, since the dancing soon converted itself into a free-for-all and more dancers were afloat than on their feet. Fortunately, everybody at the party could swim.

When the party broke up, I had no need for driving up to Chamonix to cool myself down with Mont Blanc in the moonlight. I had something else in the moonlight that I found preferable to the slopes: a girl provided specially for Erridge by Hilaire. She had been handpicked for me by Hélène Talbot, and the lady had clear and specific ideas of just what a man required.

The girl—Gerda—was beautiful. I cannot say she was as much a stunner as Mathilde de Montbard—they don't come that way so often in any guy's life—but she was far above the average. She was a northern European, healthy, and well bred. She had no repertoire of kinky performances and, if she'd had any knowledge of them, she would have been certain to disdain them. But I had no complaints. Gerda was sweet and soft and loving. Only a brute could ask for more than that.

Since Hilaire, along with the house, had taken on the de Montbard servants, he was in a position to provide the full treatment. Come morning, it was again breakfast in bed.

The manservant brought it over and served it to us. Again it was the superb croissant, the impeccable butter, the magnificent jam, and the dreamworld coffee. There was even hair of the dog for settling the previous evening's excess of champagne. Hilaire had thought of everything. We thoroughly enjoyed it. I'd expected that the lady might be embarrassed, but it was evident that the servants had neither ears nor eyes. They were no more than animated instruments for providing the creature comforts. One ignored them and took one's pleasures. Even when Mme Douvaine made her appearance to do up the flat, the lady was not nonplussed. She merely complimented me on my domestic arrangements.

Mme Douvaine was equally unruffled. She was pleased at having no shocking disorder to deal with. She made it abundantly clear that she was pleased for me: in her opinion it was high time that I had turned to a good woman. I'd had enough of the exotic with Mathilde de Montbard, and it was well that she had put a stop to that with the cross she had affixed to the door. Also, she was tired of the odor of brimstone. In her book, to save a man from damnation there was nothing like a night abed with a good woman.

Mme Douvaine had helped with the service at the party and she was eager to discuss it. She approved. It had been a good party and Hilaire was going to be a good influence in the neighborhood.

That morning all hell broke loose on the Geneva Bourse. Zurich was making its final moves. All the wild shenanigans they had been planning and about which I'd been having such strong misgivings had been put into gear. The quotations were going every which way; if they had any direction to them, it was every direction that was calculated to kick Gaspard's ass for him. The Zurichers had him with his pants down and he was taking history's most phenomenal whipping.

I went over to Geneva to take Gerda home and I stopped by the Bourse to check on how Hilaire was doing. He was riding high—but he was paying for his every success. His colleagues were looking on the good man with suspicion. The thing had gone too far to fool them. They knew the limits of possibility: no human being could be so perspicacious or so lucky. If Hilaire was not in league with the devil, then he must be operating in league with the Zurich bankers, and, for the Geneva crowd, there was no distinction to be made between the two. Both were equally nefarious.

I could work up no sympathy—the time had come for them to be regretting their association with Gaspard Lapointe. They should by now be confronted with the realization that they had been keeping bad company.

I let Hilaire take me to lunch.

The scene in the restaurant's main dining room was a picture of unmitigated pathos. Gaspard was there, stripped of his customary arrogance, standing naked to his enemies; and there was nobody to offer him any quarter. I could almost pity the son of a bitch, but I was able to go beyond that easily by reminding myself of the attitude he would be taking if he had been in Hilaire's place: he would have been luxuriating in greed.

Hilaire was in no way unhappy about the riches that were pouring in on him, but he was managing to take them with becoming grace. He deplored the envy and suspicion exhibited by his fellow bankers. Although he was powerless to do anything that might have allayed these feelings, he was being most circumspect, making no unnecessary moves that might have served to promote them. He was being the gentleman.

I spoke to Gaspard, who was making a valiant effort to dissemble the anxiety he was feeling, but it was too obviously parlous for any hope of successful concealment. We chatted for several minutes, but any reference to the morning's activities on the Bourse was studiously avoided. Our conversation was about Hilaire's party. He complimented me on my wind surfing prowess and I registered the suitable disclaimers. My achievements, after all, had been feeble when held up to comparison with those of Georges and Hilaire.

He soon switched the talk over to football. He'd heard of my attendance at the Annemasse–Annecy game. Although he made no pretense at being a football fan, admitting the while that he was probably the only living male in the area who was not, he approved of my developing friendly relations with the local citizenry. That the citizen in question happened to be the chappie who had provided the occasion for the arrest and detention of his two cohorts he wisely refrained from mentioning. One did not speak of the lower classes, and Gaspard under any circumstances was an unmitigated snob. (Even when he had been scratching, he had scratched with elegance.) That *I* had developed relations with the lower classes didn't disturb him. I was, after all, an American, and were not Americans notoriously blind to social distinctions?

Reluctantly, he pulled away from me. He had to return to the Bourse in time for the afternoon opening. That he was hoping that through his maneuverings of the afternoon he would contrive to recoup his fortunes was obvious, and I saw no need to disabuse him. He would be learning quickly enough; the Zurich bankers were assiduous teachers.

I was far too kind to hang about the exchange watching Gaspard flounder and scramble. Moreover, since Hilaire had to give his whole mind to keeping abreast of the insane manipulations, I had no wish to let myself get underfoot or to distract the man from the complicated business at hand. I went out to the golf club, but there was nobody there to give me a game. With the market standing on end, that was the least I should have expected. Gaspard, after all, was not alone.

The rescue operation Zurich had promised me they would put on for the Geneva crowd would not yet have begun. Up to this point, punishment was being meted out evenly to the lot of them. They were all on the floor of the Bourse, writhing under the lash. I could only hope that Zurich's St.

Bernards would turn up in time and that the boys would be rescued.

Meanwhile, radio reports in the club's bar had it that the exchanges in London, Paris, and even Wall Street were reeling. The Chancellor of the Exchequer was spreading the soothing unguent of his reassuring words over the House of Commons. The French ministries were deliberating. The President had called a meeting of the National Security Council and the chairman of the Federal Reserve was sitting in with them. Nicaragua and San Salvador had been shifted to a back burner. The entire world was hanging on the mad antics of the Zurichers.

I called it a day and went home to practice my wind surfing. After all, both my neighbor and Hilaire had put me to shame.

Since Hilaire was occupied for the afternoon on the floor of the Bourse, keeping his footing as successfully as he had on the surfing board, he would not be using his board. Georges had been having an afternoon at home, so he came out to join me. Not a financier, he was immune to the turmoil on the Geneva Bourse.

Georges Bardelot proved, in fact, to be unexpectedly unfeeling, deriving great amusement from the discomfiture of the banking fraternity. They were too rich, and he considered them to be ripe for leveling. Georges was sufficiently good-natured, however, to make an exception of Hilaire, and he insisted that this was not merely because Hilaire had thrown such a great party. Georges took satisfaction from my assurances that Hilaire was in there riding with the madness. He called it the reward of virtue. The fact that the wealthier Zurichers were doing well did not disturb him. He had no knowledge of that crowd. They did not come down his way or louse up his lake.

Georges and I were required to attend a further hearing into the guilt of Arnin the next morning. This was followed by a second hearing, one that took up the guilt of the two bully boys. At this one I was a witness and Guy, the young footballer, was with me. Hilaire was there as well, to testify to the theft of his billfold. The whole thing went as smooth as silk, the testimony of too many of us sterling citizens stacking up against the two goons.

Gaspard had been summoned to appear and he alone was uncooperative. He confessed to knowing the two thugs and he even went so far as to vouch for their good character. He seemed to have no realization of the fact that that he was digging his own grave. He went into a long song and dance about the two ferocious guard dogs and the armed man he kept on his gate for the security of his guests. I cannot say that Gaspard did not make an impression on the magistrates. The guy still pulled a lot of weight. But it was not enough. The evidence was much too damning.

Any further steps to be taken awaited word from the Zurichers. They would need to let me know when they had located the miserable bank official who had given Gaspard access to Henri-Edouard de Montbard's safe deposit box and that they had secured the man's written and sworn confession. I had from them their every assurance that they would get it done, but assurances were hardly sufficient to move on.

CHAPTER 10

Trusting no one, the Zurich bankers took it upon themselves to give Geneva the word. Simultaneously, they took the pressure off all the other exchanges, and the financial world settled into no more than its customary state of hysteria. The reversal, of course, had come too late to be of any value to Gaspard Lapointe. The man was ruined, stripped clean, his bones picked. Those Zurichers were nothing if not efficient.

He put his lakeside mansion up for sale. His furniture, silver, glass, and china were going to auction. The Cézannes, had at last been sent off to London to be auctioned there, and the art world was humming with the expectation of record prices. It was evident that Gaspard's hope was that the funds he was to realize from these sales would serve as the foundation for a reestablishment of his financial position. They would, of course, instead be going to his lawyers in payment for his defense. The man's ordeal had only just begun; the worst was still to come.

Unexpectedly, I found I was forced to delay making my first move against him. There were aspects of the history I would be obliged to take to the gendarmes that had never made sense. I had tried very hard to convince myself of Gaspard's unlimited power, but I couldn't make it work—the will to believe was just not sufficient. Before I would open my big mouth, I would have to get the whole thing rethought.

Going into Geneva, I took up my misgivings with Hilaire.

"The safe deposit box," I said, "is the stumbling block."

"How so?"

"Your idea that it took no more than a bribe to put the diamonds into Gaspard's hands just won't wash, my friend. It puts too much strain on the bounds of the credible."

"There could have been no other way."

"But you must know better than that. Two keys would be required for opening any box."

"Yes. One key is held by the bank and the other by the renter."

"Without the renter's key how could the thing have been possible?"

Reluctantly, Hilaire conceded that this would be a worrisome point. "Yes," he said. "By one method or another Gaspard must have come into possession of that key. Without it, bribery could have availed him nothing."

Once the two of us had been forced into a recognition of this much, the remainder became all too easy.

"The best part of this switch in our thinking," I said, "is the elimination of a lot of other uncomfortably iffy aspects. Stupid acts of unmotivated savagery are now beginning to make sense. For the first time I can begin to understand why Mathilde should have been murdered."

"Then that wasn't jealousy?"

"Oh, come on, Hilaire! How can you imagine that any man could be jealous of a lady who was so lavish with her favors? The guy would have to be insane."

"You tell me that there were the two killers. They would be the pair of bully boys—who took murder so lightly that it needn't have taken more than a moment of pique to set them off."

"I'd rather not believe it," I said, "but unhappily it's become too clear that it had to be Mathilde who instigated the murder of her husband."

"Yes. What other way could there have been to bring the key into her hands?"

"And once she had it, furthermore, she needed Henri-Edouard out of the way before she could put it to any easy use."

"Yes, Matthew, mon ami, you have the thing right, now."

"I'm wondering how I could have been so stupid. All along, I've been ignoring an important circumstance."

"Like what?"

"The de Montbard house had been ransacked. For me to have attributed that to mere vandalism was grossly insufficient."

"Certainly. They had to have been looking for something."

"I'd been assuming that it was the diamonds.

That would have meant they thought the lady was lacking in caution."

"For them to have been looking for the safe deposit box key makes far better sense."

"More than that," I said. "It now has to follow that even after they had killed for the key, they were unaware of its significance."

"Gaspard would have been the one who knew *that*, and the murder, therefore, would have been committed on his orders and for his benefit."

"They had killed Mathilde, turned the house inside out in their search for the key, found it, and in their ignorance turned it over to Gaspard."

"It need not even have been ignorance," said Hilaire. "The key, after all, would have been worthless in their hands."

"Why worthless?"

"They didn't have the power to put it to any use."

"I don't know. . . . If they didn't have the means for managing a bribe, there could have been threats or even violence. And those babies are good at violence."

"No. They would need to have known whom they could usefully threaten. This enterprise called for a man who had sufficient entree for him to know just whom he was to bribe—or threaten."

"I get it, and that would have had to be someone like Gaspard."

So he had made promises and the two killers had turned the key over to him. Once he'd had the diamonds in his hands, he had reneged on the promises. Such was Gaspard's code: contracts were made only to be broken. Seeing the thing this way made everything fall into place. And the participants were all too sane: there was nothing unreasonable about what they'd been doing.

Hilaire's gratitude was pitiful.

"You have restored my faith in Swiss banking, Matthew," he said. "I can never thank you enough."

"Nonsense," I said. "I just had to get my thinking straightened around."

"That miserable dog of a bank man who took Gaspard's bribe was bad enough, but not nearly as bad as I thought. I can breathe again now without fearing for the safety of my assets."

"Just be sure you hang on to your deposit box key," I said.

"I am going to be most careful to contrive to keep unmurdered."

I made another run up to Zurich to present my clarification to the Zurich bankers. Baby was wearing a rut in the highways between Geneva and Zurich, and my appetite for that journey was becoming much diminished.

The Zurichers now undertook seriously the mission of finding the bank man who had accepted Gaspard's bribe and of wringing a confession out of him. This would be the one piece of evidence still needed to pin things down. They weren't pretending that it would be easy. It would be necessary for them to penetrate the most secret recesses of the Geneva banking setup. They assured me, nevertheless, that they were not without the means.

"We'll find the son of a bitch," Schneider, one of the Zurich magnates, said. "And we'll bring him to heel. We'll have him talking, and he will swear to everything he will say. He will put it in writing and he will sign it."

No one was doubting that the gendarme and the murderers would be certain to spill their guts. There, after all, would lie their only hope for even some small degree of clemency. Arnin had already violated his oath of office, and in his greed he had lost for himself any support he might have from his colleagues.

"It's unfortunate," said Heiliger, another Zuricher, "that the commission of the crimes should have fallen into two jurisdictions."

Two of the murders had been done in France: that of the garbage collector and that of Mathilde de Montbard. The Henri-Edouard de Montbard killing, however, inevitably raised questions. His body had been found afloat on the garbage scow in an area of the lake which lay in Swiss territory.

"But there is no knowing that the scow with the body on it had not done some drifting," Schneider argued, "even possibly over from the French side of the lake."

"How do you propose to go about proving that?" I asked.

It was painful for them to confess that anything could be beyond the limits of their impressive powers, but they were forced to such an admission, and we were stuck with the two jurisdictions. They reminded me, however, that the robbery of the safe deposit box key had been done in France.

"But Gaspard didn't use it in France," I reminded them. "He used it in Geneva."

"So that, too . . . is a Swiss crime," said Heiliger.

"The trial procedure is going to be cumbersome."

"Necessarily," the banker said in agreement, "but there's no help for that. Is there?"

"No," answered his colleague, Schneider. "For a crime perpetrated through international collaboration there can be no just reprisal unless justice is meted out through a process of international collaboration."

"So the bastard's ordeal will be further prolonged. He will be accorded no mercy on either side of the border," said Erridge.

The Zurichers told me to return to the Lake Geneva and sit tight until they gave me the word. They would take immediate action and I was to expect progress reports at regular intervals. They were lavish in their praise of me and in their gratitude for the service I was doing, they said, for Switzerland.

"Because you have been a man of steel, Matthew, you have mitigated or possibly even wiped away the idiocy of your countrymen's interference with the earlier stage of our reprisals against Gaspard," said Schneider.

Back at the lake I filled up the waiting time with wind surfing, skiing, and attendance at Annemasse football matches. My friendship with Guy and his dad mellowed into a major plus. The kid had studied engineering, I discovered.

"It hasn't gotten me much so far," he complained.

"No job?"

"I have been bossing a road-building gang. All I can say for it is that it keeps me out in the fresh air."

"Maybe there's something I can do about that," I said. "As soon as I have Gaspard securely tucked away, I'll be going to work. How would you like to come along and work with me?"

Guy hesitated. "I'd be running out on the guys on the team," he said.

His regret was understandable.

His old man took a hand. "You should be weighing M. Erridge's offer against going on with the road-building gang," he said. "It will be a long time before you could hope for anything better around here."

That did it. We made a deal.

Zurich had told me that I could count on a few days' lull while they would presumably be accomplishing the all but impossible, and I used those days in addition for going up to Paris and getting things pinned down with Albert. I took the lad with me.

Guy was the world's complete innocent. Since he had never been anywhere, Paris knocked him over. In no time at all he and Albert were bosom buddies. Rigaud in his own time had himself been a footballer, and the boy's fame had reached even as far as Paris. They put their heads together and, before I knew what they were up to, they were laying plans for putting together a team on the Swiss job. When Erridge suggested that there would be work to do, they took to calling me a spoilsport. Albert, I discovered, was going to be a bad influence.

When we went out for a night on the town—an eye-popping night for the kid, with Montmartre, the Quartier Latin, Montparnasse, and all that jazz thrown in—I first realized just how bad an influence. I found myself playing censor and duenna, two unaccustomed roles for me, and I was uncomfortable in them. I could not, however, ignore the fact that we would be returning to Annemasse and daddy and I wouldn't relish the idea of my bringing the kid home with my having contributed to the delinquency of a minor. Actually Guy wasn't a minor, but he seemed very young to me. As his father had once put it, the lad was possibly even not too big for a whipping.

After a few days, I brought Guy back to Annemasse and the reunion with papa. He told the old man all about Paris, and greatly to my relief the old boy declared himself well pleased with the contributions Albert and I had made to his son's education.

Our return had been triggered by word from Zurich. My banker friends up there were ready to roll.

"We have located the bank official who opened the box for Gaspard," Heiliger reported, long-distance to Paris. "He wasn't easy to find, but we've had him singing and he's recorded his song on paper and signed it. When the magistrates confront him with Gaspard, he'll be hog-tied."

Having had the go-ahead signal, I paid two visits: one was to the gendarmerie in Geneva and the second to the gendarmerie on the French side. At both I was welcomed eagerly. Zurich had laid a solid foundation and I discovered that the gendarmes had been expecting me. They had already made all the necessary arrangements for international cooperation and a squad was sent out to bring Gaspard in.

Why I should have gone to the hearing armed with my loaded revolver I will never know. The gendarmes would have Gaspard in custody. And I had always had him pegged as a manipulative type, not at all the kind for any violent action.

My young footballing friend and his dad came

along, but only as spectators. I had been watching
Guy perform on the football field; now they had
come to watch Erridge go into his act, and I was
determined not to disappoint them. This was far
too important, and I had been too long building up
to it. They were duly impressed with the majesty
of the court. Your law-abiding types always will be:
for them the processes of the law must be awe-in-
spiring. It might go better for criminals if they
could be equally impressed. Surely a decent dose of
respect should act as a deterrent to crime.

Gaspard appeared, fully panoplied in his arrogance. The first of the two hearings was held by
the Swiss, and Gaspard appeared to be dismissing
the presiding magistrates as quite beneath his notice. They had never been invited to any of his galas, and everyone who was anyone had always been
on his list. The magistrates could not have been
unaware of his attitude. Even in offering them the
conventional gestures of respect he tainted his every move with contempt.

He came accompanied by a great retinue of witnesses. Most of the best people of Geneva and Lausanne were there to attest to his impeccable character and unbending honesty. He had even reached
as far along the lake as Vevey and Montreux to
bring in toadies to testify to his virtue.

"Gaspard Lapointe is a man of pure gold."

"Gaspard Lapointe is a pillar of the community."

"Gaspard Lapointe is an angel of charity."

Weighted down with such garbage, the proceed-

ings quickly became an unmitigated and burden-
some bore. This same refrain was repeated over
and over again, ad nauseam.

Clearly, Gaspard expected that Arnin and the
two murderers would add their voices to the
chorus. He most certainly expected it of the bank
executive who had taken his bribe. He had to be
thinking that the man could do no less than make
some show of gratitude. By all four of them, of
course, he was disappointed. It had become too evident to them that Gaspard was no longer the tower
of strength they remembered. Furthermore, they
were themselves out in the cold, stuck with their
various predicaments, and there would be no help
from them.

The deposition the Zurichers had extracted from
the bank executive was offered in evidence and
read into the record. For that Gaspard had not
been prepared. The reading was a bad blow, and
under it he wilted visibly.

There was, of course, much worse to come. The
gendarme, Arnin, was called to the stand. Hob-
bling in leg irons, he had to be assisted. Here was a
man who had been broken. He talked and he held
back nothing. Heedless of the fact that he was offering revelations of his own guilt that were shocking even me, he babbled. For a man who had never
had any truth in him, Arnin came up with stuff
that went way back into a past that no one had so
much as begun to suspect. His association in crime
with Gaspard had not been a new thing. He had

long served Lapointe as a conduit to the seats of power in France. Changes in government had never made any difference. Ministries might go into new hands, but the bureaucracies were indestructibly immortal and Gaspard had been holding all of those in the palm of his hand. And the testimony reached far beyond Gaspard.

Since, for this first hearing, the inquiring magistrates were Swiss, they accepted all this intelligence with ill-concealed enjoyment. There was going to be fear and chagrin in high places and they were loving it. The magistrates would be learning better soon enough: the second hearing would be French and that would do for the Swiss high panjandrums at least as much as was now being heaped upon the French.

Despite his strange lapse into honesty, the gendarme worked hard at doing whatever he could for himself.

"I was seduced," he said. "Until this villian came and cast his spell of evil on me, I was innocent. No man surpassed me in my devotion to duty. He led me astray with his blandishments."

"In other words, you accepted his bribes."

"I had no reason to believe they were bribes. Who was I to have had doubts of any acts a gentleman of M. Lapointe's eminence might have required of me?"

"The fact that they had to be secret acts did not rouse your suspicions? You were a gendarme. Presumably you had been trained in your profession."

"He assured me that I was doing nothing illegal. The secrecy was necessary for financial reasons only. Please, sirs, if your worships will, please look at the diplomats. Are they not always acting in secret?"

"You would have us take it that you considered yourself to be a diplomat?"

"That was the way M. Lapointe put it to me. How else was I to consider it?"

Whatever else Gaspard may have been, he was a shrewd psychologist. The presence of the United Nations in the Geneva area had infected even the general public. Intrigue had become indigenous.

Arnin was followed to the stand by the pair of murderers. They were dragged in similarly hobbled, and if anything they looked to be in even worse shape than the gendarme. They were taken in turn and they competed in their attempts to place the greater weight of the guilt each on the other. Arnin may have been pathetic, but this pair were disgusting. It was obvious that the gendarme could never have been the innocent he was now claiming to have been, but that couldn't change what had to be equally obvious: that Gaspard had paraded before the man all his power and influence, and with that display had seduced him.

The two testified to the fact that their connection with Gaspard had been initiated by the gendarme. In general they attempted to hold their testimony down to material that was either already entered into evidence or that otherwise was so blatantly obvious that there could be no hope of concealing it.

"It must be brought to the attention of your worships that it was in innocence that we first had contact with M. Lapointe," said one of the men—the one I knew as Gaston. "We shared . . . his bed."

In this connection, they revealed in Gaspard's noticeable start something I had not previously suspected. I'd been under the impression that he would be utterly without shame, but this was blatantly something that Gaspard preferred to have had left unknown.

"M. Lapointe had one great passion," Fernando, the second man said. "It was his pleasure to be whipped."

The two went on, in lurid detail, until the magistrates stepped in and called a halt.

"We did murder Henri-Edouard de Montbard and the garbage collector," Gaston confessed. "But those murders were all the fault of Arnin."

"It came of his stupidity," Fernando explained. "He let himself be sucked into believing that the diamonds would be in the garbage. He was so stupid that he didn't even know there were diamonds. What he told us was gold in the garbage. It was no way our fault. It was him all along."

"Killing Mathilde de Montbard," Gaston said, taking it up again, "wasn't all that different. M. Lapointe ordered us to do that. We could just as easily have stolen the key from her without murdering her, but M. Lapointe insisted."

The other lug again stepped into it. "Except for knowing," he said, "that he was going to take pleasure in it we couldn't understand why he should want the lady dead."

"If we had known," said Gaston, "he would never have had the diamonds. They would have been ours and we would have been safely off to South America. But he insisted, and in our stupidity we let him have the key. How could we know that anything so little could have so much importance?"

It was evident that the two idiots were still bemused by that thought.

Item by item, grim truth by grim truth, they dug Gaspard's grave. Fernando slipped into the silly error of saying that they had made their first mistake with me. I suppose his eagerness to talk about this arose from the fact that it was his boyfriend who'd encountered me that night just after the storm at the mouth of the footpath that ran along the castle wall. "Shooting the flashlight out of his hand served us no purpose. He was standing there, an admirable target. He could just as easily have been shot in the belly or through the heart—and disposed of on the spot."

Gaston made a try at doing himself a bit of good with that. "I let the man go on living," he said. "Killing gives me no pleasure. How could I know that he would become our nemesis? Any advantage we thought we had from using his revolver to kill the garbage collector and de Montbard was never any damn good."

It was at the French hearing that Gaspard, having arrived at a recognition of the desperate nature of his position, whipped into violent action.

How the gendarmes could have been so stupid to bring him into court without first taking the precaution of searching him certainly defies any sensible explanation. Under the circumstances, a body search would have been routine, without any concession to the supposed eminence of the accused. I could only suppose that the French, laboring under the delusion that shoot-'em-ups were an exclusively American thing, had never for a moment considered the possibility of the great Gaspard running amok.

I was never certain of his motivation. He could hardly have been deluded enough to believe that he could shoot his way out to freedom and make it all the way through the Mont Blanc Tunnel into Italy and liberty. Surely he knew that the Italians would immediately kick his tail back across the border. He was the man, after all, who was the initiating cause of their recent financial woes—and they would be slow to forget that. It seems, now, more likely that Gaspard had some idea of evening scores with the gendarme, the two murderers, the bank executive, Hilaire, the Zurich bankers, Erridge, and even the examining magistrates. That he had no skill to bring to his attempt was all too evident.

His choice of his first target was, at the least, ill judged.

He whipped out his gun and fired at the gendarme.

Gaspard couldn't have known that I would come to the hearing with my revolver, although, being French, he could have been expected to subscribe to the popular European notion that there was no American who was not congenitally gun-happy.

The shot he squeezed off at the gendarme missed, and the slug buried itself instead in the desk of one of the examining magistrates. Wood splinters flew in all directions, and throughout the hearing room magistrates, witnesses, and guards were diving for cover. Only two of the spectators were possessed of the balls it took to join the action. My Annemasse buddy and his old man, ever mindful of the assist Erridge had come up with at the time of the kid's mugging, stood with me.

I fired a single shot but was careful to hold it down to that—no more than a warning. Too many bodies were in rapid motion for me to permit myself anything more. What I'd had in mind had been to shoot the gun out of Gaspard's hand. If in the process I happened to get his hand as well, I was ready to rate that a plus. It now seemed appropriate that I should demonstrate an expertise at least equal to that displayed by the bully boy in the path by the castle wall.

There was, however, never any need for that second shot.

The Annemasse laddie dove for Gaspard's legs, took him with neat precision right at the knees, and brought him crashing down. No linebacker in the pros could have done it better. And I was astonished: tackling, to my knowledge, had never been any part of his game. Guy's old man was right in there with him. His contribution was pinning Gaspard to the floor by sitting on his head.

By slow stages order was restored. The guards took Gaspard and shackled him. With the most elaborate ceremony, the magistrates gave the thanks of the court to the three of us for our prompt and effective action. Nobody pinned any medals on us, but we weren't permitted to get away, later, without the mandatory kisses on both cheeks. Meanwhile, the remainder of the session was stormy: Gaspard had been shackled, but he wasn't gagged—and he was in excellent voice.

The time came for pronouncing sentence. The law fell most heavily on the killers, who were condemned to life imprisonment. Arnin, the gendarme, fared slightly better: for him it was thirty years and loss of his pension. For Gaspard it was also thirty years, but with the possibility that good behavior might win him a parole. That wound the whole thing up.

After a celebratory dinner at Le Père Bise—a farewell party that I threw for the Annemasse chappie and his father, Hilaire, my neighbor Georges from the lake, and myself—I wrapped it up. Before we left for Paris, Guy and I went up to

Zurich, where we pinned down the final negotiations on the dam contract. After that it was to the City of Light and Albert for a last fling before the three of us would be coming back to the work site in the Bernese Oberland.

What with Hilaire, Mme Douvaine, the kid's dad, and my neighbor left behind us, we three were kept well informed on how well Gaspard was doing in confinement. Prison suited that worthy all too well. Settling in, he quickly established himself as the jail's biggest operator. It wasn't long before he was taking his fellow prisoners for everything they had. That was Gaspard. He won them all.

Whenever he might be coming out on parole, he would be emerging possessed of the means for reestablishing himself as the kingpin of Geneva finance. He would again be a force to reckon with. Hilaire was already trembling in anticipation of the consequences.

"Gaspard," he told me on my return to the lake a few months later, "would most certainly be out for revenge."

"You can't still be afraid of the man, Hilaire."

"But I can, Matthew. I am. Every visiting day I go to the prison. Gaspard is still what he always was."

"Is he behaving himself?"

"He is, and most admirably. I have been cultivating the men on the parole board and promoting their granting him his parole."

"Hilaire, that's idiotic! You can't have been doing it."

"But I have, Matthew. When Gaspard comes out, he will come owing me a heavy debt."

The Zurichers, however, were made of sterner stuff. Schneider and Heiliger and I were at the Café zur Kronenhalle.

"His offenses are unforgivable. We shall not forget," said Schneider.

"He will be coming out," I said, "free on parole —or haven't you heard?"

"We have heard, and it will be thanks to Hilaire and his craven stupidity. Unhappily, we are going to be unable to prevent his reestablishing a great financial position. But we are determined to do what we can to diminish it."

"That isn't what has poor Hilaire terrified," I said.

"Yes. Hilaire Talbot fears the day when Gaspard might reinstate himself in his position of banking power. That, however, is the one thing that we can prevent, and you may be assured that we shall prevent it. We have him stripped of all his influence."

"But will he remain stripped?"

"On that you have our guarantee. We will be indebted to you if you will tell Hilaire Talbot as much, from us."

About the Author

Aaron Marc Stein graduated from Princeton with a degree in classics and archaeology. His first novel was published on the recommendation of Theodore Dreiser. He has published nearly one hundred novels in the Crime Club, a body of work for which he has received the Mystery Writers of America's Grand Master Award. Mr. Stein has chronicled the adventures of Matt Erridge in such previous novels as *The Bombing Run, Hangman's Row,* and *A Body for a Buddy.* Mr. Stein lives in New York City.